Sabotage at Sports City

Joe nudged Frank and pointed out one of the athletes on the Chinese team, warming up on the gymnasium floor. "That's Kyung Chin," Joe said. "He's probably the best amateur gymnast in the world."

Suddenly Joe's view was blocked by his friend Chet, who was running up the bleacher steps. "My cousin Sean is dropping out of the Olympics—for real," Chet said, panting hard.

"Why? What happened?" Frank asked.

"There's been another death threat," Chet explained.

Joe sat back, stunned. How could one nut try to close down the Olympics? That's what would happen if the athletes started packing up and going home. Just then Joe noticed Kyung Chin approaching the high bar. The gymnast's energy was focused entirely on the bar.

Kyung jumped on the springboard and flew up to the bar, ten feet from the floor. But as Kyung's hands grabbed the bar, he fumbled awkwardly and slipped. The gymnast yelled angrily in Chinese as he fell to the floor.

"No!" Joe called out involuntarily as he watched Kyung collapse, hitting the safety mat face first!

The Hardy Boys Mystery Stories

Available from MINSTREL Books

115

The
HARDY BOYS®

SABOTAGE AT SPORTS CITY

FRANKLIN W. DIXON

A MINSTREL® BOOK

PUBLISHED BY POCKET BOOKS

New York   London   Toronto   Sydney   Tokyo   Singapore

A MINSTREL PAPERBACK *ORIGINAL*

A Minstrel Book published by
POCKET BOOKS, a division of Simon & Schuster Inc.
1230 Avenue of the Americas, New York, NY 10020

Copyright © 1992 by Simon & Schuster Inc.
Front cover illustration by Daniel Horne

Produced by Mega-Books of New York, Inc.

ISBN: 0-671-73062-2

First Minstrel Books printing August 1992

10 9 8 7 6 5 4 3 2

Printed in the U.S.A.

Contents

SABOTAGE AT
SPORTS CITY

1 Olympic Threat

"USA! USA!" The roar of the crowd was deafening. Seventy thousand voices surrounded Frank Hardy and rocked the modern outdoor stadium. Frank could hardly hear his own voice above the thousands of fans who kept shouting, "USA! USA!"

"Hey, Joe!" Frank yelled, trying to be heard above the crowd. He waved to his brother from the middle of the fifth row. "Over here!"

Frank and Joe looked unmistakably like brothers. Both had athletic builds and were dressed casually in jeans and T-shirts. Frank, at six-feet-one, was an inch taller than his brother and had dark hair and eyes. Blue-eyed Joe was the more muscular of the two.

1

As he stood in the aisle at the end of the row, Joe Hardy flashed an envelope and gave Frank a thumbs-up sign. Then Joe started moving toward his brother, crossing in front of people while trying not to step on their feet. His blond hair bounced over onto his forehead as he moved.

Usually seventeen-year-old Joe and eighteen-year-old Frank spent their free time solving crimes in the East Coast city of Bayport, where they had earned reputations as hot young detectives. But for the next two weeks, the Hardys were going to forget all about crime solving. Right now they were a thousand miles from home, attending the summer Olympics.

"What events did we get tickets for?" Frank asked.

"I don't know. I haven't looked," Joe said, holding on to the envelope as though it held a couple of thousand-dollar bills. "Chet just handed me the envelope and took off. He was acting pretty strange."

"Really?" Frank said, raising one eyebrow. "I wonder why."

Frank and his brother were watching the Olympics thanks to their best friend, Chet Morton. Or more precisely, thanks to Chet's cousin Sean O'Malley, a marathon runner who lived in Ireland. Right after New Year's, Sean had written to Chet's parents, telling them that he was coming to the United States that summer. Sean was a marathoner for the Irish Olympic team. A few weeks later, he sent Chet tickets to the opening ceremonies and promised to get more tickets for other events. When Chet's family couldn't go, Chet invited his best friends, Frank and Joe, to go instead.

"Do you believe this?" Joe shouted, tearing open the envelope and staring at the first ticket in the stack. "Front-row seats for basketball!"

Frank smiled with anticipation. "What else?"

"What else?" Joe said. "Who cares? I mean, Russia, Brazil, Germany—everybody's going to get a lesson in how to play hoop, American style. And we're going to see it from the front row!"

Frank understood his brother's excitement. Joe was an all-round athlete, and basketball was one of his favorite sports.

Joe flipped to the next set of tickets. "Check it out!" he cried. "Gymnastics! And here are the track tickets." Joe studied the tickets for a moment and then consulted a program listing all the Olympic events. "We'll be in the stadium for the decathlon around the time when the marathon is finishing. We'll get to see both events at the same time."

"Cool," Frank said. The decathlon was one of Frank's favorite competitions—ten different track events held over a period of two days. But of course the marathon was the most important event they had come to see, since Chet's cousin was competing in it.

"Think Sean will win the gold?"

3

"I don't know. Chet must have told me about a hundred fifty times on the plane that no runner from Ireland has ever won the marathon," Frank said. "But they say Sean has a good chance of being the first."

Joe turned his attention to the field. The largest international band he had ever seen was marching in formation. Filling the field were dancers wearing sequined costumes, waving streamers, and carrying multicolored flags. Finally the Olympic athletes from each nation began to enter the field from the far end of the stadium. As they paraded around the track, the athletes waved to the crowds, who waved and cheered back. Each group of competitors wore a different uniform. The United States had on blue nylon jackets and red and white nylon pants. Another country's team wore red turtlenecks. One athlete from each country was carrying the flag of that nation.

"Looks like the United States sent more than two hundred athletes," Joe said to his brother.

Frank pointed to a small group dressed in brown and gold. "Yeah, but Luxembourg sent only two."

"If it's their basketball team, they're in major trouble," Joe said with a laugh.

Frank laughed, too. "Yeah, but seriously, the important thing is just to be here."

"And we are, big brother. We are!" Joe exclaimed.

"Hey—there's Chet," Frank said, spotting his

large-boned, brown-haired friend. Joe looked over and saw Chet Morton standing at the end of the aisle. He was holding three ice cream sandwiches in one hand and a large drink in the other. He was trying to work his way toward Frank and Joe. But there wasn't much legroom in front of the spectators, and Chet's size didn't help.

"Excuse me. Excuse me," Chet was saying as he made his way down the row.

He set off a chain reaction with every person he walked past. One by one, the spectators shouted, "Ouch!" "Hey, watch where you're stepping, pal." "Get off my foot!"

Joe laughed and poked Frank. "The games haven't even started yet, and he's setting an Olympic record for stepping on people's feet."

"At least he's bringing us ice cream sandwiches," Frank said, laughing. "I'm starved."

When Chet finally reached them, he handed Frank the large drink. "Hold this," he said. Frank held the soda while Chet opened all three ice cream sandwiches. Then he put them together, making one gigantic triple decker, and took a bite.

"Those are all for *you?*" Frank asked, his mouth falling open.

"Oh, did you want some?" Chet asked. "Sorry."

Chet nervously gobbled down the ice cream mega-sandwich, but Frank and Joe could see that he didn't seem to be enjoying it one bit. And when Chet didn't enjoy his food, it was a sure sign that something was wrong.

"What's the matter?" Frank asked, still holding the soda. Chet took the drink and downed it in almost one chug before answering.

"It's Sean," Chet finally said, nodding toward the field.

"Which one *is* Sean, anyway?" Joe asked.

"He's the one with carrot red hair," Chet said, pointing toward the group of athletes who had just come onto the field. "And he's wearing sunglasses with one blue lens and one red lens. They're his trademark."

Joe scanned the athletes as the Irish team marched by. He picked Sean out immediately. His bright red hair stood out in the crowd like a ball of neon cotton candy.

"Frank, Joe," Chet said, wiping his mouth with his hands. "Sean's scared. Scared for his life. From what he told me, the whole Olympics could be ruined."

The words made Joe turn away from the field and focus all his attention on Chet. "What's the story?" Joe asked.

Chet lowered his voice. "The word has leaked out that the chairman of the Olympic Committee got a letter today. It was a threat against all the athletes. It said, 'I plan to set an Olympic record—fifty-three people will die during these games!'"

"It's a sick joke," Joe said. "It's got to be a joke from some nut case."

"Sometimes those nut cases aren't kidding," Frank said seriously. "How'd you hear about it, Chet?"

"I was talking to Sean a little while ago, before his team marched out onto the field. The Olympic Committee told him and all of the other athletes to be super careful," Chet explained, "and not take any chances."

"But they're taking a chance every time they go on the field," Joe said. "Every one of the events is a security nightmare."

Joe wasn't thinking like a sports fan anymore. His detective instincts had taken over, and Chet knew it.

"You're right," Chet said slowly. "They're all in danger—including my cousin."

Frank and Joe looked at each other and then grew silent while the crowd around them seemed to grow happier and louder. After the teams paraded once around the track, they all stopped in straight rows at one end of the field. Everyone was waiting for the Olympic torch to arrive.

"Did the note say anything about how they would die?" Joe whispered to Chet.

Chet shook his head. "It just said they'd die."

"It could be a whole team," Joe said tensely. "If it is, they might as well be wearing bull's-eyes on their uniforms."

7

"We should find out which country sent fifty-three athletes. It's probably some kind of political threat," Frank said.

"The officials already thought of that," Chet said. "But no go. The only country that comes close is Canada, with fifty-two."

"Let's talk to Sean right after the opening ceremonies," Frank said to his brother. "Maybe he can tell us something more."

Just then a voice came over the public address system. "Ladies and gentlemen," said the announcer, "the Olympic flame is about to enter the stadium. This flame was lit from the original Olympic flame that burns eternally in Athens, Greece, birthplace of the first Olympic Games. It has traveled around the world, passed from athlete to athlete. In another moment the Olympic torch in our stadium will be lit with this flame. It will remain burning until the games of this Summer Olympiad are over."

Joe looked toward the far end of the stadium and watched a young woman in white running clothes come trotting onto the track. As soon as the crowd saw that she was carrying the small torch with the flame, they burst into cheers and applause.

"I wonder if she knows about the threat," Joe said.

"Hard to tell," Frank replied.

"Yeah. Well, I kind of hope she doesn't know," Joe said. "I mean, what a great moment—to be

8

lighting the Olympic torch. It's really a bummer to have the shadow of some kind of crazy threat hanging over it."

The young woman ran once around the track. Then she headed toward a young man who was dressed identically, in white shorts and an Olympic shirt. He was standing at the foot of a long stairway that rose to a platform at the top of the stadium, three stories above the field.

As she passed him the torch, there was another cheer from the crowd. Then he started jogging up the steps to the giant Olympic torch—a gleaming silver bowl twenty feet across, resting on a broad silver pedestal. At the top, the runner turned to face the crowd. He held the small torch out to them as a salute. And then he turned back to the huge silver torch, letting his small flame rest at the edge of the huge bowl.

Suddenly an enormous ball of red fire blasted out of the bowl, as if the runner had ignited a stick of dynamite. Flames leaped up toward him, and the entire stadium watched in stunned silence. The suddenness of the explosion knocked the torchbearer off his feet and sent him tumbling right down the long flight of stairs behind him!

2 In Deep Trouble

"It's started!" Joe shouted, jumping up. "That guy's the first of fifty-three!"

Joe watched, frozen, as the torchbearer plunged backward, falling seventy-five feet down the treacherous stairs. A moment later the runner lay in a lifeless heap at the foot of the long stairway.

The red blaze of flame blasted up from the Olympic torch for only a few seconds. Then it sank below the lip of the bowl and died. Thick black smoke rose and spread slowly over the stadium like an evil shadow.

Nearly everyone in the stadium jumped up to see what had happened. Almost immediately, other athletes rushed to help, and for a moment it

10

was impossible for Joe to see what was happening. A security patrol car zoomed onto the field, followed by a medical unit. Finally the runner stood up and limped from the field.

"We've got to talk to Sean, and fast," Joe said. He and Frank locked eyes, and they both understood what the look meant—they were on another case!

Chet pulled a small automatic camera from his pocket and took a picture of the event. "That runner could have been killed," he said as he looked over the scene. The opening ceremonies continued, but the festive mood had clearly been broken. The spectators seemed eager to get out of the stadium, away from the black smoke that still hung in the air.

Joe looked up at the media booth at the top of the stadium and wondered what the television announcers were saying about the explosion. "We'd probably know more about what's going on if we were watching this on TV," Joe said.

"You're right," Frank agreed, glancing up at a helicopter. "That chopper has the best view," Frank observed. "It's transmitting its signal back to the broadcast center."

As soon as the ceremonies were over, Frank, Joe, and Chet walked through the Olympic village. Sports City was a collection of Olympic offices, sports facilities, and dormitories for the athletes. The whole complex covered about twenty square blocks. The stadium was within walking distance of all the downtown restaurants and hotels, including the one where Frank and Joe were staying.

"Look at all the security guards," Joe said, nodding toward one of the dormitories. "There's someone posted at every single door."

"Yeah, and I'll bet there will be *two* guys on every door by tonight," Frank said.

After they had taken a quick tour of Sports City, they walked to a burger joint called the Track Meat. Chet had already arranged to meet Sean there. The Track Meat was mobbed when they arrived. Athletes and visitors from nearly every country in the world were talking and eating together. But Sean was nowhere to be found.

When they finally sat down, Frank, Joe, and Chet ordered burgers and watched TV coverage of the Olympics on a giant-screen TV. There was a video replay of the torch exploding in flames, followed by an interview with an Olympic official who explained that it was an accident. He said it was caused by a small clog in the natural gas jets supplying the torch.

"An accident? Tell me another story," Joe said to the television.

"You mean you don't think it was an accident?" asked a voice behind them.

Joe turned to see a guy with a wiry, muscular body and a thick shock of red hair. As he sat

12

down at the table, he pulled off a pair of sunglasses with one red lens and one blue lens.

"Sean!" Chet exclaimed. "Hey, Frank, Joe—this is my cousin."

"How's it going?" Frank asked.

"I've been better," Sean replied. "Nothing like coming to the Olympics and getting a death threat. Most of the athletes are freaking out."

Sean's voice was gentle and had a thick Irish accent. But Frank could sense tension in his steel gray eyes.

"How about you?" Frank asked.

"I'm scared, but I've trained too long to let it stop me," Sean said. "I want my chance at a gold medal. Still, I wish someone would catch the guy who sent that note. Chet tells me you guys might be able to do that."

"Maybe," Frank said. "We'll need more information first. Tell us everything you know about the note."

"I didn't see it," Sean said, "so I can't help you out much. Tell me something. Why don't you think what happened in the stadium today was an accident?"

"Because the Olympic flame is natural gas," Joe said. "There had to be oil of some kind in the torch bowl to make black smoke like that. Just enough to make a lot of smoke and noise and then die down quickly. I figure this was a warning."

"See. I told you these guys were dynamite

13

detectives," Chet said proudly. "Are you going to get on the case?" he asked Frank.

"I don't know," Frank said. For a minute he was quiet as he thought about the note. The question he couldn't stop asking himself was, Why fifty-three? Why that particular number? Were there fifty-three countries represented? He reached for his official Olympic Games souvenir book, hoping to make the connection. Were there fifty-three different events? "Oh, no!" Frank blurted out.

"What?" Joe, Chet, and Sean all asked.

Frank didn't want to answer. "Nothing. It's a coincidence, probably. I just noticed how many runners are entered in the marathon event."

Sean's face turned pale. "He's right," he said. "I forgot. Fifty-three, including me . . ."

"It's just a theory," Frank said. He was sorry that he had mentioned the clue in front of Sean. "We don't know anything for sure."

"Listen," Joe said. "We *are* going to get on the case, super fast. If it could have anything to do with the marathon, we want to help. And when Frank and I are on a case for a friend, nothing slows us down."

Sean tried to smile. "Is there something I can do to help?"

"We could use some official credentials," Frank said.

"Know anyone in security?" Joe asked.

"I'll ask my coach," Sean said.

"Great," Joe said. "Meanwhile, stay cool and don't worry about the threat."

Sean stood up, nodded, and put on his trademark sunglasses. "Gotta go, lads," he said. "I've got to get in a six-mile run. Nice meeting you. And thanks for your help."

When Sean was gone, Chet decided he wanted to take a shuttle bus tour of the Olympic sites where other events were being held. Many of the biggest events—such as track, basketball, gymnastics, and swimming—were being held in Sports City. The rest of the events were spread out around town.

Frank and Joe went along on the shuttle bus tour, but found themselves talking about Sean and the torch incident the whole time. They hardly noticed their surroundings. When the tour was over, the three all went back to the hotel and ordered food from room service. The Hardys were sharing a room, and Chet was staying in his own room, down the hall.

"First thing tomorrow, let's call Sean," Frank said. "Maybe he'll have those security credentials by then."

But the next morning, Sean didn't answer his phone.

Chet started to get worried. "You guys take the tickets and go on to the Olympics," he said. "I'll head for the athletes' dormitories to see if I can find him."

While Chet went to look for Sean, Frank and

Joe hurried toward their first Olympic event, women's springboard diving. It was in the new pool building, right next to the one that housed the gymnastics events.

But as they approached the tall, gleaming, white concrete building, Frank stopped. There was a crowd at the entrance but no one was going in. Frank heard people muttering, talking angrily to each other, and shaking their heads. Whatever was going on wasn't very popular with the crowd.

He and Joe squeezed their way toward the entrance, where they found signs taped across the glass of each door: All diving and swimming events have been canceled because of pool maintenance.

Frank took one look at his brother, and they both shook their heads.

"No way. The pool can't need maintenance the day the Olympics begin," Joe said.

Frank nodded. There was definitely some kind of trouble. "Let's see if we can get in, anyway," he said, motioning for Joe to follow. They quickly walked around to a side door of the building. A similar sign was posted, but there weren't any guards watching the door. Frank took a chance and pulled on one of the door handles, expecting it to be locked. It wasn't. They quietly slipped inside.

Not more than five seconds later, Frank heard a voice call out. "Excuse me," a woman said, coming up behind them. "This is a restricted area."

The name on her official Olympic badge read Cathleen Barton. The badge also said Olympic Security, and from all of the other code words and numbers, Frank figured she was pretty high up in the organization. "Why were the events canceled?" he asked her.

"Pool maintenance," Cathleen Barton replied. "You'll have to leave now." She was an attractive tall woman, about forty years old. Her short black hair had one dramatic streak of white in front.

"What kind of maintenance?" Frank asked.

"The pump," she said with a nod of her head.

Joe didn't let it rest a beat. "What's wrong with it?" he asked.

"It's not pumping," she said sharply. "Please leave now."

"Hey, we can fix it," Frank blurted out.

Joe gave Frank a quick look of surprise and then pulled a straight face. "Uh, that's right," he said. "That's what our dad does. He installs and maintains pools."

"It's under control," she said.

"Oh, I doubt that," Joe said, darting past her and toward the doors leading to the pool.

Cathleen Barton ran to catch up with Joe, and Frank followed both of them.

"Hey, Frank, take a deep breath," Joe said.

Frank did, and immediately felt a sharp pain in his lungs.

17

Joe flashed his blue eyes at Cathleen Barton. "I know that smell," he said. "It's chlorine, and it smells as if someone dumped about a thousand times too much of it in the pool. We're talking major eye damage and skin burns if anyone jumps in that water, aren't we, Frank?"

"Absolutely," Frank said. "Listen, Ms. Barton, nobody wants fifty-three people to die."

Cathleen Barton flinched at the statement, but she wasn't about to give in. "You'll have to leave," she said nervously. She looked around and started calling to a maintenance worker, a man in tan coveralls. "Lyle! Lyle!"

Lyle was a big man who had a sunburned face and long black hair in a ponytail. "Miss?" he said, not moving. He was big but he looked harmless.

"These guys are in a restricted area," Cathleen said. "Get them out of here right now."

As soon as Lyle started walking toward them, Cathleen turned around and left. She obviously thought Lyle could handle the situation.

"Cathleen said we should ask you if someone knew how all the chlorine got in the pool," Frank said when Cathleen was gone.

"Yeah?" Lyle said. He looked confused. "I thought she said to get rid of you."

"We're helping security," Joe said, ignoring his question.

"Huh?" Lyle said. "That's weird. Does she know you're with security?"

Frank jumped to help out Joe. "Cathleen's

trying to railroad us, Lyle. But we know you'll help us. What did you see?" he asked, crossing his arms in front of him.

"Not much. About five this morning, I saw a guy leaving."

"What did he look like?" Joe interrupted.

"Blond guy. Athlete—I could tell from his body. Blue bikini trunks with a red stripe on the sides and a white T-shirt. He was carrying something that was covered up with a towel. It looked like some kind of plastic bucket or bottle."

"Something that could have contained chlorine?" Frank asked.

"You got it," Lyle said.

"Did you get a look at his face?" Joe asked.

"Nope. He was wearing swim goggles." Lyle looked back at the pool. "Gonna take hours to drain the pool and fill it again. Doesn't make sense."

Lyle shrugged, and Frank and Joe walked back outside the pool building. Joe gave Frank a "Now what?" look.

"Talk about not making sense," Frank said. "If the fifty-three people who are supposed to die are marathoners, then why put chlorine in the pool?"

"All I know is that this thing must be big," Joe replied. "Really big. It could be some sort of huge terrorist plot. International, maybe."

The idea sent a chill shooting down Frank's back. He didn't even want to consider it.

19

Suddenly Frank felt something else on his back. It was a hand—tapping him hard. He turned and saw a security guard standing behind him, looking serious.

"You Frank and Joe Hardy?" the guard asked.

Frank nodded.

"Then come with me," the guard said. "I've been looking for you."

Uh-oh, Joe thought to himself. Now we're in deep trouble!

3 High Risk on the High Bar

"What did we do?" Joe mumbled under his breath to his brother.

Frank shrugged and continued to walk briskly. From the look on the guard's face, they were in major trouble. It wouldn't be the first time he and Joe had gotten into trouble for sticking their noses into places they weren't supposed to.

Without saying another word, the guard led them to the small modern office building a short distance from the pool. The gold lettering on the front door read Olympic Security. They passed a security checkpoint, then took some twists and turns down narrow hallways. Finally they arrived at a heavy wooden door with a sign that read

Director of Security. The guard gestured for Frank and Joe to go into the large office.

Inside, behind a large walnut desk, sat Cathleen Barton. She had three telephones on her desk, along with a half dozen walkie-talkies sitting in their rechargers. There were no windows in the room, Frank noticed. In fact, there were no windows in the entire building, he realized. Everything looked a little green in the glare of the fluorescent lights.

"All right, Bernie. You can go," Cathleen said, waving her hand.

When the guard had left the room, Cathleen put her hands on the desk and faced Frank and Joe. "I should have guessed it when we met earlier," she said.

"Guessed what?" Joe asked.

Cathleen ignored Joe's question and went on. "Then I heard about a request for credentials from an Irish marathoner," she said. "So I did some checking on you two. The information just came in a minute ago." She unfolded a computer printout. "Why didn't you guys say you're Fenton Hardy's kids?"

Joe was shocked. "You know our dad?"

"What kind of security chief would I be if I didn't know a veteran detective like Fenton Hardy?" she replied. "Besides, I helped him out on a case of his about ten years ago." Cathleen finally broke into a smile. "I haven't talked to him since then, until I called him today. He told me all

22

about you guys. But I told him what I'm about to tell you. I can't afford to have you guys blabbing or getting in the way."

"Yeah, but . . ." Joe started to say.

"You must be Joe," she said, interrupting him. "Your dad said you wouldn't let me finish a sentence."

Frank laughed, and Joe sat back and sulked.

"He pointed out that you guys could be useful to us. You're young and you look like a couple of athletes, so you'll blend in. I thought about it and I think he's right. Maybe you can help us out."

She opened a desk drawer and tossed two blue cards and two orange cards, each sealed in plastic, onto the desktop. "The blue ones are athlete ID cards. The orange ones are security IDs. If you get into trouble, or need something special, flash the orange cards," she said. "Otherwise, the blue ones should get you into just about any building in Sports City."

"Great!" Joe leaped out of his seat, sweeping up the cards.

"What happened with the Olympic torch yesterday?" Frank asked, getting right down to business.

"We found traces of oil in the bowl," Cathleen said. "But I think it's a dead end. About five thousand people had access to the torch before the games started."

"Why so many?" Frank asked, surprised.

"It took hundreds of carpenters just to build

23

those platforms alone," Cathleen explained. "And about two thousand singers, dancers, and musicians had to rehearse for three days before the opening day. Plus the athletes are permitted to come into the stadium at any time."

"Okay, what about the chlorine in the pool?" Frank asked.

"We've done some checking and turned up nothing. But you're welcome to give it a try. Of course, the FBI is working on it, too. They're on the whole case around the clock."

"Could we see the threatening letter that was sent to the Olympic Committee?" Joe asked. "It might have some clues."

Cathleen gave them a small smile. "Sorry, guys. That much involvement you can't have. The FBI took the note, and their people are examining it with every high-powered microscope and tool they've got. I *can* let you look at a copy of it."

She reached into her drawer and pulled out a photocopy of the letter.

Joe glanced at the page. The words on the letter were typed or computer-printed—Joe wasn't sure which. But the note looked pretty standard, and it said just what Sean had reported: I plan to set an Olympic record—fifty-three people will die during these games! "Can we keep this?" Joe asked.

"Sorry again," Cathleen said. "The FBI is keeping this case so tight, I can't even let you have this copy. I don't know what good it would do you, anyway. If there are any real clues, they're in the original paper itself—or in finger-prints. The bureau will handle all that."

"Right," Joe said, disappointed.

"Well, what are your ideas?" Frank asked Cathleen. "Do you have any suspects?"

"So far, we figure it's some kind of political terrorist threat. It's the most likely explanation. But I'm open to any theories you've got."

"Tell her yours, Frank," Joe said.

Since Cathleen looked interested immediately, Frank explained, "There are fifty-three runners in the marathon."

Cathleen's face dropped, and she shook her head in concern. "We hadn't thought of that," she said. "I sincerely hope you're wrong. We can't protect fifty-three different people over a twenty-six-mile race. No security force is that large. And the course winds through all kinds of neighborhoods in the city. Snipers could be on top of buildings or mixed in with the crowds. Those runners would be easy targets."

"Well, we may be wrong," Joe said. "It may be some other fifty-three athletes. Or maybe even fifty-three fans."

Cathleen shuddered. "I don't know which would be worse," she said. There was a silence as the three of them imagined all the possibilities. Then Frank and Joe got up to leave.

"Let's hope this is all just an ugly practical joke," Cathleen said, walking them to the door.

On the way out, Cathleen gave them a special phone number to call in case of emergencies. "Check in regularly," she said. "Let me know if you find anything at all. Oh, and one last thing. Don't say a word to the press about the note or any of this. We're asking all the athletes to keep it quiet. Mum's the word."

"No problem," Frank said, closing the door behind him.

"Where to?" Joe asked.

"I say we find Lyle again and see whether we can get some better leads on the guy who put chlorine in the pool," Frank said.

Joe nodded and led the way back to the pool building. It took only a few minutes to find Lyle. He told them that since the main pool was closed for maintenance, the swimmers were practicing at a nearby community college. Frank showed Lyle his orange security ID card, and Lyle agreed to help them out.

The three of them took an Olympic shuttle bus to the community college. Once they got there, they sat in the bleachers, looking down on the swimmers doing their grueling workout.

"Tell us if anyone looks familiar," Joe said.

"You've got it, Sarge," Lyle said, leaning back on the bleachers behind him. Ever since he'd seen their ID cards, Lyle had been calling them both Sarge. "But it won't be easy. I told you, Sarge, he was wearing a white T-shirt this morning."

"Watch how they walk, or how they hold their heads. Use your imagination," Joe said.

"Uh-huh," Lyle said, nodding slowly. The look on his face was as good as a confession that he had no idea what Joe was talking about.

"Hey, there's the guy!" Lyle cried out suddenly, pointing down at the pool area. "That's him!"

Frank and Joe hurried down the bleachers, heading for the guy Lyle had pointed to—a very tall swimmer who was relaxing by the pool in a yoga lotus position. He was wearing a swimming cap on his head, so it was impossible to know what color hair he had.

"Could we ask you a question?" Frank said.

"Yes, but my English is not very good," the swimmer said. He spoke with a thick German accent.

"We'd like to know where you were early this morning, around five o'clock," Frank said.

"Five o'clock this morning? I was in the exercise room with my team members and my coach."

"Oh," Joe said, with a disappointed frown. If the swimmer was telling the truth, he'd also just eliminated five other swimmers and one coach. "Thanks."

"Sure," said the swimmer, taking off his cap and shaking out his short black hair.

"I don't believe it," Joe said as they walked away. "The guy didn't even have blond hair. We're wasting our time with Lyle."

Frank walked back to the bleachers and tapped

27

Lyle on the shoulder. "Let's go," he said. "You've got a real talent for picking out people with rock-solid alibis."

"Sorry, Sarge."

Frank and Joe left the building in silence. Joe could see from the look on Frank's face that his brother was pretty frustrated with how little they'd learned so far.

"Hey, cheer up, Frank," Joe said. "I just realized something. None of those swimmers have much hair at all. Some of them even shaved their heads to cut down on resistance in the water."

"So?"

"So I don't think the guy Lyle saw this morning is an Olympic swimmer after all."

Frank smiled. "I knew I was related to you for a good reason," he said, giving his brother a slap on the back.

After grabbing a quick lunch, Joe and Frank found Chet and went to the Olympic gymnasium to see the first day of men's gymnastic competition. On the way, Chet told them that he had spent the morning trying to reach Sean—with no luck.

"Well, keep calling his dorm room," Joe said. "Don't worry. He'll turn up."

"Boy, we sure are early," Chet said as they entered the gymnasium. "The athletes aren't even here to warm up yet."

Frank, Joe, and Chet found their seats, which

28

were in the middle of the twenty-third row. From there, they could see just about every corner of the gymnasium. They also had a good view of all the equipment, including the large blue mat in the middle of the gym for the tumbling exercises, the tall, shiny high bar, and the squat pommel horse. The equipment was already set up, and workers were placing safety mats under everything.

"Looks like we have the place to ourselves," Frank said. He sat down in his seat and draped his legs across the seat in front of him.

"I think I'll go call Sean again," Chet said, heading back down the stairs. "That way I can check out the snack bar at the same time."

Joe laughed and shook his head. "That's what I like about Chet. He's predictable." He turned his attention back to the floor and saw that the German and Chinese gymnastic teams had arrived and were warming up.

Joe nudged Frank and pointed out one athlete on the Chinese team. "That's Kyung Chin," he said. "He's probably the best amateur gymnast in the world."

Joe watched Kyung warming up on the floor mats for a few minutes. But suddenly his view was blocked by Chet, who was running up the steps, out of breath and empty-handed.

"He's going to do it," Chet shouted, shaking his head and panting hard.

"Who? What?" Joe asked.

"Sean," Chet said. "He's dropping out of the Olympics. For real."

"Why? What happened?" Frank asked.

"He wouldn't tell me," Chet said, "but his roommate, Bryan Dorset, got on the phone. He's a British marathoner, and he sounded even more nervous than Sean. He said there's been another note. Only this time it was sent to him and Sean, personally."

"What did it say?" Joe asked eagerly.

Chet shrugged. "They wouldn't tell me anything. They just said they'll meet us at the Track Meat in an hour."

Joe sat back, stunned. How could one nut try to close down the whole Olympics? That's what would happen if athletes started packing up and going home. His eyes moved down again to the floor of the gymnasium, where Kyung Chin was approaching the high bar. Joe could see the concentration on his face. The gymnast's energy was focused entirely on the bar. Joe focused, too, trying to push everything else out of his mind. This was an incredible moment. Joe was actually watching one of the world's great athletes.

Kyung jumped on the springboard and flew up to the bar, ten feet from the floor. Watching him made Joe think of a bird lifting off the ground effortlessly, gracefully. In another split second Kyung would reach out to grab the high bar and his whirling exercise would begin.

But as Kyung's hands grabbed the bar, he fumbled awkwardly and slipped—blowing the move like a total amateur! The gymnast yelled angrily in Chinese and started to fall to the floor.

"No!" Joe called out involuntarily as he watched Kyung collapse, hitting the safety mat face first!

4 Dead Last

Kyung Chin lay groaning on the mat. Frank quickly figured out why. His leg was twisted under him in a hideous contortion.

Frank, Joe, and Chet scrambled out of the stands and onto the floor. Quickly, Chet pulled out his camera and took a picture of the scene. But no one seemed to notice them because Kyung's trainers and coaches—along with athletes from both the Chinese and German teams —were crowding around. The word had spread to media people outside the gymnasium, too. Frank saw TV camera crews, guys with microphones, and press photographers swarming in.

While everyone asked Chin what had happened, Joe turned his attention back to the high bar. What *had* gone wrong? Joe had a hunch, but he had to test it out first.

He grabbed a white towel off the bench. Then he ran leaping onto the springboard with every ounce of his strength.

Joe arched, arms outstretched, toward the high bar with the towel in one hand.

For a moment the surprised crowd and camera crews hushed and watched Joe as he spun around the bar twice. His arms were locked straight, one hand gripping the bar, the other hand holding on with the towel. Finally Joe let go, landing on the safety mat and bending his knees for the dismount.

Everyone else in the crowd turned back to Kyung Chin, but Frank and Chet hurried over toward Joe.

"What were you doing up there?" Frank asked.

Joe didn't answer. Instead, he showed Frank and Chet the towel. The white cloth was stained with light brown blotches.

Frank held the towel to his nose and sniffed. "Oil," he said to Joe.

Joe nodded and wiped his oily hand on the towel. "I know," he said. "No wonder Kyung slipped."

By now, Kyung Chin was being helped off the floor, hobbling in pain. The reporters were heading over to Frank, Chet, and Joe.

"Come on," Frank said. "Let's get out of here before these guys start asking questions about us, or about that towel. We don't want the whole world to know that we're working on this case."

"Right," Joe agreed. "Besides, we'd better report this to Cathleen Barton."

The two brothers grabbed Chet by the arm and sped out of the arena. They stopped at a phone booth and called the direct phone number Cathleen Barton had given them.

"You guys are doing good work already," she told Joe, sounding pleased. "Drop the towel off at the front desk of my office building. We'll have it checked out, and I'll let you know if we turn up any clues."

They dropped off the towel at the security office and headed over to the Track Meat to meet Sean. By the time they got there, news of Kyung Chin's fall had already hit the airwaves. Sean and another athlete were watching news coverage of the accident on the restaurant's giant screen TV.

"Oh, hello, lads," Sean said when he saw the Hardys and Chet walking toward his table. "This is my roommate, Bryan Dorset."

"Hi," Bryan said with a shy smile.

Frank shook hands with Bryan, who was lean and muscular like Sean. Bryan had curly black hair under his souvenir hat, which had a collection of Olympic pins stuck all over it.

"Bryan, these are the American detectives I told you about," Sean said, continuing the introductions. "You already know my cousin Chet."

"Detectives, eh?" Bryan said in a crisp British

accent. "Well, I hope you can figure out what's going on around here," he said. "I've got a meeting with my coach. Gotta push off." He stood up to leave.

"See you later," Sean called as his roommate left. Then he turned back to Frank and Joe. "He's a funny duck," Sean said. "Doesn't say much, but he's a great guy. Did you hear about Kyung Chin?"

"We were there when he fell," Frank said.

"They say he's going to compete, anyway," Sean said. "Sprained ankle and all. It'll probably kill him on the landing. That's courage."

"You've gotta be tough to compete," Frank said.

"Yeah, well, not me. I'm out of here," Sean said.

"How come?" Frank asked.

"There's really nothing to talk about," Sean said. "I mean, I thought this would be my year. I thought I really could win. But I'm not going to get my head blown off for a gold medal."

"Start from the beginning," Joe said. "What happened?"

Sean pulled a folded piece of paper out of his sweatpants pocket and flipped it across the table to Frank. "This was slipped under my door," he said.

Frank unfolded the note and read it aloud. "Drop out of the marathon unless you want to DIE! Each marathon runner will be murdered

35

following the race—in order. The gold medalist will be murdered first . . . the silver medalist second . . . the bronze medalist third . . . and so on. Even the runner who comes in last will be dead eventually. Dead last.''

"Every runner in the marathon got a copy of that note," Sean said. "All fifty-three of us."

Frank swallowed hard. Finding out his theory was right didn't make him happy.

"Keep the letter," Sean said, pushing his chair away from the table as if he wanted to leave. "A souvenir of the Olympics that didn't happen for me."

"Come on, Sean. You can't—you don't want to . . ." Chet couldn't finish his sentence.

"If I win the race, my prize is I get killed *first*, get it?" Sean snapped. "No thanks."

"You know," Frank said, thinking out loud, "this letter tells us a lot more about this guy than we knew before." That got Sean's attention, as Frank knew it would.

"At first I thought there were only two probable suspects," Frank went on. "Now I think there could be three. The first and most logical suspect is some political terrorist group. I don't think that's the case, because there were no demands made in the second note, either, which is what terrorists usually do. Suspect number two is some nut who wants to sabotage the Olympics."

"Like, Mr. Blue Bikini Bathing Suit with the

Red Stripe," Joe said. "The guy who dumped the chlorine in the pool."

"Right," Frank agreed. "Even though we know what he looks like, it won't be easy to find him. But this new note builds a case for suspect number three—someone who mainly wants to ruin the marathon race."

"What?" Sean's gray eyes opened wide.

"I'm serious," Frank continued. "It's possible that whoever sent the first note to the Olympic Committee did it to get your attention. And the torch and the chlorine in the pool—maybe those were just warnings, too. Small acts of sabotage to make all the athletes nervous. If you look at the evidence, this note will have one more main effect. It'll scare off the competition in the marathon race, right? I mean, you're thinking of quitting, aren't you? It's working already."

Joe nodded in agreement. "How were these notes slipped under your door, anyway?" he asked Sean. "It had to be someone who knows which rooms the marathoners are staying in."

"That could be any one of the athletes," Sean said. "We *all* got a list of every athlete attending these games. That's how they sent out the dorm room assignments—on a long computer printout. It has the names and room numbers of every athlete in Sports City."

"It could be anyone," Joe said. "But if Frank's right, then, it's a marathoner. Can you think of anyone, Sean, who might do something like this?"

Sean looked around the room before his eyes came back to Joe's. Rock music from the jukebox drowned out his voice. He had to say it twice. "Sure. I can think of someone."

"Really? Who?" Joe asked. "Tell us everything."

"There's a French runner, Maddox Pomereau," Sean said. "We call him Mad Dog because he's crazy. He likes to mess with people's heads before a race. He has a history of playing pranks on other runners."

"What kind of pranks?" Frank asked.

"Oh, stealing a guy's best shoes from his locker. Or paying people to stand in the crowd and boo a particular runner—things like that. Some people even say he arranged to give all the other runners food poisoning in a race in France last year. But these latest tricks are too much, even for him."

"Maybe so," Frank said. "Maybe I'm totally wrong."

"You weren't wrong with your marathon theory," Joe pointed out.

"We'll check out this Mad Dog Pomereau," Frank said. "Maybe he's not guilty and maybe he is. But I do think we have a chance to solve this case before the race."

"Sure!" Chet exclaimed. "See? With these guys on the job, there's no reason to quit." Chet lowered his voice. "Especially now that they're

38

working undercover for the Olympic Committee."

"Okay, okay," Sean said. He moved back toward the table and even tried to smile. "I'll wait. What are you guys going to do?"

"Talk to Mad Dog," Frank said. "When's the best time to catch him?"

"Tomorrow morning," Sean said. "But be ready to run six or seven miles."

The next morning, Frank got up at dawn and woke his brother. The two of them quickly dressed in running clothes. They caught up with Sean as he was running with about a dozen other athletes through the hills outside the Olympic village. It was part of the same route that would be used when the marathon race was actually run. The runners wanted to check out the course, while keeping in shape. Fortunately for Frank and Joe, they were only going to run seven or eight miles, not all twenty-six.

Frank jogged along next to Sean, trying to match his pace.

"Is Mad Dog around?" Frank asked.

"You can't miss him," Sean said, jerking his head sideways.

Frank looked around and caught a quick glimpse of a runner in neon blue spandex running shorts and a pink T-shirt. Then he noticed the guy's thick, collar-length blond hair. How lucky can we get? Frank thought to himself. At least on the surface, Mad Dog matched the description of the guy who had dumped chlorine into the pool.

The only problem was that Frank couldn't get a look at Maddox Pomereau's face—because he was walking on his hands! It was hard to see his face when he was upside down.

If anyone is a Mad Dog, this guy definitely is, Frank thought.

"Sean," Mad Dog called out loudly from twenty yards away. *"Mon ami*, I'm thinking of running the marathon on my hands just to give you a little bitty chance of winning." He laughed so hard that he lost his balance, tumbling over onto his feet.

"Frank and Joe Hardy," Sean said coldly, slowing to a jog and then stopping completely, "Mad Dog Pomereau."

Instead of shaking Frank's hand, Mad Dog kept his hands on his hips. His smile was broad, but his eyes were challenging.

"Would you mind if we asked you a few questions?" Joe asked.

"You guys reporters?" Mad Dog asked.

"No, just a couple of guys who ask questions," Frank said.

"It is a beautiful morning, so ask away," Mad Dog said, giving Sean a quick wink.

"Do you have a blue bathing suit with a red stripe?" Frank asked.

Mad Dog shrugged. "I have many bathing suits."

Frank and Joe exchanged a look. "Were you at the Olympic pool yesterday morning?" Joe asked.

"I am not a swimmer," Mad Dog said.

Frustrated, Frank tried another topic. "What do you think about the threat against the marathon runners?"

"I think it's a shame," Mad Dog said. "It will ruin the race for me. I will have no one to race against if everyone is too afraid to run."

"You're not afraid?" Joe said.

Mad Dog smiled again. "People can be afraid of many things in this world, but I would not allow anything to stop me from winning the gold medal."

All of a sudden, Sean spoke up. His face was tense with anger. "Maybe you're not afraid because you know *you* won't be hurt," he said.

"And how could I possibly know that?" Mad Dog said. "The threat was made against all of us."

"Maybe you're not afraid," Sean said, "because *you* sent that note to us to play with our heads."

Mad Dog laughed loudly. "Playing with your head, *mon ami,* is like playing with the air."

Joe could see that Mad Dog had pushed Sean's detonator. Sean charged at Mad Dog, grabbing for a handful of the runner's pink shirt. But Mad

41

Dog dodged him and then quickly gave Sean a solid push in the chest. Sean stumbled backward, tripping over a fat tree root and falling down a steep dirt embankment.

Sean cried out as he tumbled backward over the rocky ground. When he came to a stop, his face was twisted in pain. He was holding his ankle, and his face was turning red. "I think you just broke my leg!"

5 Celebrity Lunch

Joe half ran and half slid down the embankment to reach Sean. Frank came panting right behind him.

Back at the top, Mad Dog called out, "Sean, are you okay?"

"Okay?" Sean shouted. "I can't move my leg—I'll bet that sounds okay to you."

"Forgive me, *mon ami*," Mad Dog called. "I didn't know you were so lightweight."

At the bottom of the slope, Joe found Sean holding his leg and rocking slowly. The runner was in obvious pain.

"Oh, look at me now," Sean moaned. "I've really done it this time!"

"Don't move," Joe said. "Just stay put."

43

"What can I do to help?" Mad Dog called down.

"You can break your neck and drop out of the race!" Sean shouted. "Get out of my sight!"

Joe looked up the embankment to see Mad Dog shrug and walk away. Then he turned back to Sean. "If we lift you really carefully—"

"Is he gone?" Sean interrupted, looking up the hill.

"Yeah, he's gone," Frank said.

Then Sean began to laugh.

"What's so funny?" Joe asked.

Sean simply jumped up and trotted up the slope. "Mad Dog isn't the only one who can play psychological games on people."

Joe's mouth fell open. "I don't believe it," he said to Frank. "You mean he's okay?"

"Looks that way," Frank said.

Joe shook his head and both brothers laughed. They ran to catch up with Sean, who had already reached the top of the slope.

"Hey, Sean, wait up! What's the big idea?" Joe said, jogging along beside him.

"Oh, nothing much," Sean said with a twinkle in his eyes. "It's just that sometimes it pays to be a bit of a storyteller, you know? We call it being 'full of the blarney' back home in Ireland. Now Mad Dog will think I'm not a threat because I can't run my hardest."

At that, Sean took off at full speed, leaving Joe and Frank far behind.

44

"Hey," Sean called, turning around and running back toward them for a moment. "After training, why don't you find Cousin Chet, and we'll grab some lunch in the Sports City cafeteria?"

"Great idea!" Frank and Joe both cried out.

"See you at noon," Sean said. Then he turned around and sped off down the road.

The athletes' cafeteria was a sprawling modern space with windows on three sides. It was set on a hill and had a view of the Olympic torch and stadium. When Joe, Frank, Chet, and Sean walked in, the place was packed with wall-to-wall muscle. Gymnasts, basketball players, decathlon athletes, cyclists, archers, equestrians, and more were all eating and talking in a scramble of languages.

Even though it took forever to get through the food line, Joe wasn't impatient. He was enjoying himself keeping one eye on the food and keeping the other eye out for famous athletes. I wonder if the people here think I'm an Olympic athlete, too, Joe thought. He picked up a salad labeled Decathlete's Delight because it had ten ingredients in it. "Does any decathlete actually eat this?" Joe muttered.

"I don't know. You should ask that guy over there," Frank said. He was pointing with his head in the direction of a handsome young blond man sitting by himself at a table.

45

"Who's that?" Joe asked.

"Adam Conner, America's best chance for a gold in the decathlon."

They paid for their food and walked past the tables, looking for a place to sit. "Today was the first day of the decathlon," Frank said when they finally found a table. "There are five events today and five more tomorrow."

"How's Conner doing?" Chet asked.

"Great, so far," Frank answered. "He won the hundred-meter dash and the four-hundred-meter dash easily. The high jump was supposed to be his weakest event. But he took that, too. Beat the record by an inch and a half. Guess what else— they say he's ambidextrous. He can jump with either his left or right leg. The guy is an unstoppable machine."

"You sure know a lot about him," Joe said.

"I've been reading about him ever since Chet said we were coming to the Olympics."

"So what are his chances on day two?" Chet said through a mouthful of mashed potatoes.

"He's got great upper-body strength and fast legs," Frank said. "He'll be strong in the hundred-ten-meter hurdles and fifteen-hundred-meter run. Discus and javelin throw should be no problem. Pole vault—that's a maybe. Anyway, we'll get to find out. We've got tickets, remember?"

Sean had been quiet through the whole conversation, but then he spoke up. "You'd better not be watching the decathlon too closely," Sean said with a familiar twinkle in his eye. "Because tomorrow afternoon is the marathon, you know. Round about two o'clock I'll be leading the pack into the stadium. And I want to hear you screaming your heads off for me."

"You're positive you want to run?" Joe said.

Sean nodded. "You chaps convinced me. I just can't drop out, threat or no threat. But I'd be a mite happier if you solved this mystery before the race tomorrow."

"We're back on the case as soon as we finish lunch," Joe said, eating more quickly.

The four went back to devouring their lunches. After a few minutes, a tall, trim woman came up to their table. "Hello, Sean," she said with what sounded to Joe like a Swedish accent.

"Hello, Sigrid," Sean said. "Long time, no see."

"I stayed away from the Olympic parties this year, you know that," she said, tossing back her straight, shoulder-length blond hair. "Sean, there is a rumor that Mad Dog started a fight with you. Did you get hurt?"

"It's just my ankle. It won't keep me from running," Sean said. He flashed a sly smile at Frank and Joe.

"Well, if you're thinking of making a formal protest, forget it," she said. She practically spit the words out. "You'll never get any justice from the Olympic officials. They don't know the meaning of the word." With that, she turned and walked away.

"Who was that?" Chet asked. "And what's her problem?"

"Sigrid Randers-Perhson," Sean explained. "She's a swimmer from Norway. I got to know her four years ago. Things didn't go so well for her at the last Olympics."

"Why not?" Frank asked.

"She entered the four-hundred-meter freestyle event and came in last," Sean explained. "Sigrid claimed that it wasn't her fault. She said the girl in the next lane interfered with her during the race."

"How?" Chet asked. "By splashing water in her face?"

"No," Sean said, laughing. "She claimed that the other athlete came too close to her lane and kicked her on one of the turns. The videotapes of the event didn't back her up."

"She made a formal protest to the Olympic Committee?" Frank asked.

Sean nodded. "The committee decided against her. She's been carrying a grudge ever since."

"How big of a grudge?" Joe asked.

"What's that supposed to mean?" Chet asked.

"Well, I just got an idea," Joe said slowly. "Listen—all along, we've been thinking it was a man who dumped the chlorine in the pool. But what if it wasn't? What if it was a female swimmer?"

Frank went on full alert. "You're right," he said. "If she was wearing a T-shirt over her bathing suit, from a distance she might look like a guy in a pair of bikini trunks."

"She'd fit the description," Joe said.

Frank smiled. "Good thinking, Joe. We've been so focused on Mad Dog, we've forgotten to add people to the suspect list. Sigrid definitely sounds like a candidate."

Just then Joe caught a glimpse of a guy walking up to Adam Conner's table. He was wearing a blue dress shirt, necktie, a blue blazer, and dress pants. Except for the clothes, the two guys looked exactly alike.

"Wait a minute," Joe said, giving his head a shake. "Am I seeing things? Look over there."

"Yeah. You're seeing things," Frank said with a laugh. "You're seeing Adam's twin brother, Cory. He used to be a track and field star, too."

"Both of them?" Chet asked.

"Uh-huh. They even used to enter meets together," Frank explained.

"Used to?" Joe said.

Frank nodded. "About three years ago, Cory got tangled up with a hurdle in a race and went down. He smashed up his knee and never came back."

"Hurdles, huh? I can relate," Joe said. "As much as I love track, I've never been able to run hurdles." He watched the twin brothers sitting across from each other, talking seriously. "I bet it's tough on Cory, being out of the action."

"Save your pity," Sean said. "Cory's become a TV sports analyst, covering track and field events. He's probably making more money than all of the athletes put together."

"Uh-huh," Joe said. But he was only half listening. He'd just noticed Maddox Pomereau leaving the cafeteria. "Come on, Frank," he said, quickly getting up from the table. "Let's roll."

Frank stood up. "Catch you later, guys. We just spotted Mad Dog."

"Watch out for rabies!" Sean called after them.

Frank laughed as he and his brother followed Pomereau out of the cafeteria. Up ahead, the marathoner crossed a long, squat building of cinder blocks painted pale pink. A sign on the door read Olympic Training Center. Frank and Joe gave Mad Dog a few seconds' lead and then entered the building after him.

Inside, Frank gazed at the vast space filled with every kind of gymnastic and bodybuilding equipment he'd ever seen. Weight-lifting machines, rowing machines, stationary bicycles, and benches of every kind were in use. Young men and women ran around the track that circled the gym. On one side, there was a boxing ring. The place was filled with the smell of sweat and the sounds of hard work.

"Do you think you can tail Mad Dog yourself?"

Frank asked Joe. "I'd like to stick around here to see if there's anyone else worth checking out in the gym."

Joe nodded and silently followed Mad Dog, who ducked into the men's locker room.

Frank took a quick tour around the gym, keeping his eyes and ears open. Over by the boxing ring, a young American boxer was sparring with his coach—both physically and verbally.

"Take that, you turkey!" the boxer shouted. "Ha! Gotcha that time, dough-face!"

Frank had to laugh, since the boxer was right. The short, pudgy coach did have a rather shapeless face.

Suddenly the boxer stopped moving and yelled at his coach. "Don't tell me how to stand!" the boxer shouted.

"You'll do what I tell you to do!" the coach shouted back. "And you'll call me *coach*—not *turkey*."

Frank turned to a woman standing next to him. "Who's that?" he asked.

"Charles Morgan, American heavyweight boxer," she said with a Russian accent. "They call him Chili Pepper." She laughed a little when she said his nickname, and Frank had to admit the name seemed fitting.

"Look, man," Chili Pepper said, standing over his coach, "this is a boxing glove, right? I'd be nuts to call it a hat. I call 'em as I see 'em. So I'm not going to call a *turkey* a coach!"

51

The coach's face turned red with anger. "Chili," he said, "I've already knocked you off the team and made you an alternate, because you broke training five times last week. Are you looking to get kicked off the team altogether and sent home?"

"I warned you!" Chili shouted, waving his big red glove at the coach. "If you don't put me back on the team, you're going to pay for it."

Frank couldn't believe he was hearing an athlete actually threatening his coach.

"Everyone's going to pay for it!" Chili Pepper shouted to the entire facility.

Everyone? Frank thought. Everyone at the Olympics? What did he mean? Would Chili go as far as pouring oil in the torch or chlorine in the pool? Frank stared hard at the boxer. Was this the guy who was trying to sabotage the Olympics?

Meanwhile, inside the locker room, Joe was trying to look inconspicuous. He was tracking Mad Dog, but Mad Dog wasn't leading him anywhere. Joe walked up and down the aisles, looking at the rows of lockers. Some of them were locked with padlocks, some weren't. Joe tried to stay an aisle or two away from Mad Dog, so he wouldn't be seen.

Finally Joe heard Mad Dog open a locker door. Joe walked on tiptoe to the end of the aisle and tried to make a mental note of which locker Pomereau was using. Joe couldn't quite catch the number, so he tried to memorize its position in the line.

A moment later, Mad Dog closed the locker and headed out to the huge training room. Great, Joe thought. Now's my chance. But which locker is it? There was only one in the row that didn't have a lock on it. Joe opened the locker and started looking through it.

Shoes . . . clothes . . . deodorant . . . a jump rope . . . boxing gloves . . . Joe was silently naming the things he saw inside. Wait a minute. A jump rope? Boxing gloves? Weird stuff for a runner to have.

All of a sudden, a strong hand grabbed Joe around the neck and squeezed—hard.

"What are you doing in my locker, turkey?" a voice behind Joe growled.

Joe spun around and looked into the angry face of a boxer—all 220 pounds of him. It was Chili Pepper Morgan!

6 Knocked Out Twice

Joe stared at Chili Pepper Morgan as if the boxer's massive body had just been lowered in front of him with a crane. Chili looked like a building made of muscle. He was tall and broad shouldered, but his body tapered to twenty-eight inches at the waist. His arms were thick and solid. He was still holding Joe by the neck. And Joe was starting to get just a little worried. The guy looked mad. Really mad.

"Just what do you think you're doing, turkey?" Chili yelled, squeezing Joe's neck a little tighter.

"Nothing," Joe gasped. "I was just looking in my locker."

"Oh, yeah?" Chili grunted. "Unless I'm wrong —very wrong—this is *my* locker."

"Hey, I just made a mistake, so back off, okay?" Joe said, giving Chili a light shove.

Out of nowhere and faster than Joe could believe, Chili's right hand flew out and tagged Joe on the cheek. The blow knocked him backward, and he hit his head on the locker door.

"Are you crazy?" Joe shouted, getting back on his feet.

"That's the first thing you got right, bozo," the boxer said, unleashing another right hand.

Joe swerved, and the fist missed him this time, but he felt the breeze from it. He got his balance back and prepared to dodge the next blow.

Suddenly Joe heard a loud, metallic clatter that made both him and Chili freeze. Joe looked at the end of the row of lockers to see Frank standing there. He had just slammed a locker door to get their attention.

"What's going on?" Frank yelled.

"You want some, too?" Chili yelled back, shaking his fists at Frank.

"Hold on! Hold on!" Suddenly Chili's coach came running into the locker room. He placed himself between the boxer and Joe. "What kind of trouble are you causing now?" he yelled at Chili.

"This guy was going through my locker," the boxer replied. "You know what's been going on around here—those threats and all that trouble. I thought this punk might be the guy who's responsible."

"I wasn't doing anything!" Joe shouted. "I was just looking for something, but I got the wrong locker."

"I don't know what this is about," the coach said to Chili. "But it looks like this guy made an honest mistake." He turned to Joe. "And I'm sure Chili is sorry he punched you."

Frank moved toward them. "Excuse me," he said. "May I ask a question? How long has Chili Pepper Morgan been on the alternate list?"

"Since two days before the Olympics started," the coach answered. "Why?"

"Just curious," Frank said.

Chili Pepper glared at Frank. "You better be more careful," Chili said, shaking his fist at Joe.

"Go put some ice on that eye, son," said the coach. "You're going to take home a souvenir shiner from the Olympics."

Joe and Frank left the locker room before Chili could take another swipe at Joe.

"Chili's coach is right," Frank said. "We'd better get some ice on that eye."

"Right," Joe said, touching his eye lightly. "Let's head back to the hotel."

Within a few minutes, Frank and Joe were back at the hotel, where they collected ice from the machine in the hallway near their room. Once they got to their room, Joe spotted a glimpse of himself in the mirror. His right cheek was puffy and red already. His eye looked even worse.

Frank wrapped ice cubes in hand towels. Joe placed them on his face as lightly as he could until his eye and cheek felt numb.

"Well, I blew it with Mad Dog's locker," Joe said. "Did you find out anything in the gym?"

Frank explained what he'd heard about Chili being an alternate on the boxing team. "I heard Chili arguing with his coach and threatening that everybody would be sorry if he didn't get back to box for the United States," Frank said.

"'Be sorry'"? Joe asked. "Do you think this guy might want to ruin the Olympics?"

"Could be," Frank said. "Chili was taken off the team before the Olympics started. I figure he had a reason to sabotage the games, even from the opening ceremonies."

Joe slumped back in the chair and turned on the TV. "I feel as if we're not getting anywhere in this case," he said.

Cory Conner's handsome face came into focus. "This is Cory Conner with an exclusive report. So far the excellent competition and spirit of these summer games has been marred by the explosion of the Olympic torch and the injury to Chinese gymnast Kyung Chin. We showed you dramatic footage of Kyung, right after his fall. I have just learned from my exclusive sources of a serious threat that may cover the entire Olympics with a dark cloud. I have learned that a threat has been sent to each and every runner in the Olympic marathon, a threat to their lives. Details are sketchy, and Olympic officials will not comment. But I'll stay on the story and bring you another report as soon as I can. Back to you, Jim."

Frank listened for another minute to the anchorman's commentary about how awful the threats were and what a jinx there seemed to be at the Olympics this year.

"How'd they get that story?" Joe asked. "Cathleen Barton said they weren't going to talk to the media."

"I know. She'll probably have a stroke when she sees this," Frank said.

"Seriously," Joe said. "How did that guy find out about the note? Just who are his exclusive sources?"

"There's only one way to find out," said Frank. "Let's go talk to him."

"And right now," Joe said, grabbing some more ice.

The Hardys left their hotel and hurried toward the broadcast center, which was located at the center of the Sports City complex.

"Let's keep a low profile, if we can," Frank said to Joe when they got to the lobby. He pulled out his blue athlete's ID card instead of the orange one. "We'd like to see Cory Conner," he told the receptionist.

"Take a seat on the second floor in the waiting area," she said, nodding toward some elevators.

Frank smiled at Joe.

"Piece of cake," Joe said, smiling back.

But getting to see Cory Conner wasn't so easy. In fact, after they had been in the waiting room for about an hour, it began to appear impossible. Everyone who walked by seemed to have a different answer for why Frank and Joe couldn't see Cory.

"He's busy." "He's writing his next story." "He's on the phone." And all of them sounded like excuses.

Finally, just when Frank was really losing his patience, he saw Cory Conner come walking down a long narrow hallway toward them. Cory looked exactly like his brother, and even more handsome than he did on TV.

"I'm Cory Conner," he said, shaking Frank's hand. "I understand you guys were asking to see me," he went on. His voice was smooth, but Frank thought he seemed a little ill at ease. "I've got to go on the air in a minute. What can I do for you?"

"I'm Frank Hardy and this is my brother, Joe."

"What happened to you, Joe?" Cory interrupted, staring at Joe's black eye. "Eat a knuckle sandwich for dinner?"

"Yeah," Joe said, but he didn't laugh as much as Cory did.

"We saw your report a little while ago about the threats to the marathoners," Frank said.

"You did? Great!" Cory exclaimed. "And—?"

"And we wanted to know how you found out about the note to the marathoners," Frank said.

"But I didn't say it was a note," Cory said, looking at Joe and Frank more carefully.

"But we know it was," Joe said. "We've got a friend who's going to run in the race—if he doesn't get too scared and quit. We're trying to make sure that doesn't happen."

"I understand," Cory said, checking his watch. "Guys, I haven't been in this business very long, but long enough to know rule number one: don't divulge your sources. If I told you, I wouldn't have any sources left after that."

"The Olympic Committee didn't want anyone to know about the threats in the first place," Joe said.

"Of course not," Cory said. "But I've got to report what's really happening here. That's my job."

"Will you let us talk to your source? Or ask him to contact us?" Frank asked. "He may know something that'll help us."

"No can do, fellas. Sorry." Cory checked his watch again. "I've got to go." He left them standing in the waiting room.

"Check my face," Joe said. "I feel like I just got another black eye."

Frank laughed. "Yeah—that was a knockout punch. He was no help at all."

Suddenly, a voice from behind startled them.

60

"This is Cory Conner with another Olympic exclusive."

Frank and Joe whirled toward a big-screen television set in the waiting room. There was Cory Conner, on camera from a studio. Apparently he had just walked down the hall and gone right on the air. Joe reached over and turned up the volume.

"Misfortune has struck the Olympic village again," Cory announced. "We have just learned that an athlete, a marathon runner, was involved in a hit-and-run accident earlier this evening."

"Who? What?" Joe asked out loud. Could it have been Sean?

The photo of a young man appeared in a box over Cory's left shoulder. "British runner Bryan Dorset was out on a training run when he was struck by a car. The driver did not stop. Dorset has been taken to a nearby hospital, where his condition is listed as serious."

"Bryan Dorset!" Frank cried. "That's Sean's roommate!"

7 Going for the Gold

"I can't believe it. I can't believe your roommate was hurt in a hit-and-run accident," Joe kept saying to Sean as they rode in the cab to the hospital.

"He seemed like such a nice, gentle guy," Frank said. "Last guy in the world anyone would want to hurt on purpose."

"He was," Sean agreed. Then everyone was silent for a while.

As soon as the Hardys had heard the news about Bryan Dorset, they had rushed over to Sean's dormitory to pick him up. Then they tried to call Chet at the hotel. But no one had seen Chet since noon, when they had all eaten lunch together in the Sports City cafeteria.

"Do you think this has something to do with the threats to the marathoners?" Sean finally asked.

"Maybe yes, maybe no. I'm just hoping Bryan will be able to tell us what happened," Frank said quietly.

Finally the cab pulled up in front of Sisters of Mercy Hospital. Frank rushed to the desk and quickly got Bryan's room number. Then he, Sean, and Joe hurried to Bryan's room. Bryan was lying in bed, connected to three tubes and two monitoring machines.

"Bryan, lad," Sean said. His voice was filled with concern.

Bryan didn't answer. The only sound was the rhythmic electronic *beep-beep-beep* of the vital-signs monitor.

"I'm okay, Sean," Bryan finally said in a weak voice.

Frank and Joe stepped in behind Sean and pulled up chairs near the white metal bed.

"Nothing broken," Bryan said. The shock made talking an effort. "Internal bleeding. Bruises and scrapes. I'm out of the race." Those words brought tears welling up in Bryan's eyes.

"Can you tell us what happened?" Frank asked.

"I was running, and this white car came in front of me. I couldn't get out of the way."

Frank knew he had to try getting some information from Bryan before he drifted off to sleep. "Did it come straight at you?" he asked.

"No," Bryan said. "Swervy."

"Did you see the driver?" Joe put in.

Bryan shook his head no.

"Get the license plate number?" Frank asked.

Bryan's eyes were closing as he shook his head again. "It started with a Z," he mumbled, and then he slept.

Outside in the hallway, Frank thought about Bryan's answers. "What do they add up to?" he asked Joe. "A weaving car—sounds as if the driver was out of control."

"Bryan didn't see the driver," Joe added. "So that's a wash. A letter Z in the license plate. That means the car was rented. Not much to go on."

Sean leaned back wearily against the wall in the hallway. "I don't know how you guys can be so calm at a moment like this," he said.

"What are you going to do?" Frank asked softly. "Are you still going to run in tomorrow's race?"

Sean looked toward Bryan's room before answering. "Yes, I am," he finally said. "I owe it to Bryan. He wasn't going to quit, was he? And I'm not, either!"

The next afternoon, Frank sat with Joe and Chet, feeling almost swallowed up by the noise of the crowd in the Olympic stadium. Fifty thousand people cheered and waved flags in the stands.

The marathon was already under way on the city streets. Down on the field, the second-day decathlon events were taking place. The 110-meter hurdles and the discus were over. Adam Conner had won both.

"Way to go!" Frank cheered each time Adam Conner aced another event.

"He's so close to winning the gold," Joe said, getting excited along with Frank.

"If he does well in the pole vault, he's got it nailed," Frank said. "The pole vault is his only remaining weak spot."

A wave of excitement spread through the crowd as the final decathlon events began on the field. At the same time, both the women's hundred-meter race and the javelin event were also taking place on the field. Whenever the action slowed down, the crowd turned its attention to the marathon. The entire twenty-six-mile race was being shown on one of two giant video screens in the stadium.

Frank, Joe, and Chet had watched carefully as the runners threaded their way through the hills surrounding the city. Now Frank checked his watch and realized that it was almost two o'clock. Sean had said that was when the front-runners would reach the entrance to the stadium.

A moment later, there was a hush, as if nearly

all fifty thousand spectators saw the same thing at once. A motorcycle with a camera mounted on it came into view, and up above, a helicopter that transmitted its signal down to the broadcast center appeared. The crowd watched the video screens—and the entrance to the track—waiting to see which runner would enter the stadium first. From the television coverage, it was clear that Sean and Mad Dog Pomereau were out in front, followed closely by an African runner named Sabata Khumalo and an American, Mike Stevens.

"But who's actually leading? Sean or Mad Dog?" Frank said. "From the way the cameras are covering it, I can't tell."

"Me neither," Chet said, sounding tense.

Frank didn't know where to look next. Down on the field, the decathletes were warming up to do the pole vault. Adam Conner was bending and twisting, swiveling at the waist, limbering up for his next attempt at Olympic history.

Finally a loudspeaker announced Conner's name. Adam picked up the long pole and went charging down the field. At the last possible moment, he planted the pole in the ground and leaped into the air, letting the snap of the pole hurl him upward and over the bar. The crowd applauded politely, knowing that this was only his first of many jumps. Each time he succeeded, the bar would be raised a little higher. Many more jumps would come before a winner would be declared.

Just then the announcement the spectators were waiting for was made over the public address system.

"The marathon runners are approaching the stadium," a deep voice declared.

Suddenly it seemed to Frank that his heart was beating faster, but maybe he was just picking up the beat of the stomping feet and chanting crowd.

Everyone's eyes were glued to the giant video screen. There were only two runners out ahead of the pack—Mad Dog and Sean. Mad Dog was in the lead, his legs moving fluidly, his face angry. Behind him, only four feet back, Sean was gaining on him inch by inch. Sean's face tightened and his legs kicked faster. He was closing in on the lead.

"He's going to do it!" Chet shouted. "He's going to pass him!"

A moment later Sean pulled ahead. The runners were just outside the stadium as Sean pulled away. Strong and steady, Sean pushed himself about ten feet ahead of Mad Dog and everyone else.

But as Sean ran into the tunnel leading into the stadium, something incredible happened. Mad Dog put on kick. Legs pounding hard, as if the first twenty-five miles didn't count, he ran until he caught up with Sean again!

Side by side, the two runners entered the stadium. The crowd erupted—standing and cheering and screaming—the moment they saw them. The tension and excitement were overwhelming. No one had ever seen a marathon race that was so close at the finish, with two runners neck and neck up until the final moments of the race.

Chet was standing up along with everyone else. He was yelling and clapping and calling out, "Come on, Sean!"

Frank cried out, too, standing up on the bleachers to get a better look. For a moment, both Sean and Mad Dog held on. They were making the final lap around the track, both pushing to maintain the front position.

And then suddenly everyone in the stadium stood up on the bleachers to try to get a better view. With all the jumping, shouting, pushing, and shoving, Frank was having trouble keeping his balance. But it didn't matter. All he cared about was keeping his eyes locked on the two runners.

At the far end of the track, they made the final turn. There was only a quarter-mile straight stretch to the finish line.

"Come on, Sean!" Frank screamed, along with Chet and Joe.

Sean and Mad Dog were side by side, running in perfect unison—only a hundred yards from the finish line.

Frank craned his neck to see over the crowd. Chet was standing beside him, jumping up, spilling his soft drink, and shouting his lungs out.

Then suddenly Frank felt something he hadn't expected. It was a hand in the middle of his back, giving him a quick, hard push.

Before he could grab onto anything or anyone, Frank fell forward, tumbling headfirst down the steep bleacher stairs!

8 Instant Replay

In that same instant, Joe lost his balance, too, and went twisting and diving into the crowd of people in front of him. The fans were screaming and clapping as the marathon runners approached the finish line. But all Joe could see were feet and legs as he went down. Then he felt a sudden sharp pain as his head struck concrete.

The world started spinning around. Joe shook his head hard to try to keep from blacking out. When things finally slowed down, he saw Frank a few feet away, dazed and blinking with surprise.

"What happened?" Joe asked his brother, touching the back of his head where he was starting to get a huge lump.

"I don't know," Frank said. "One minute I was watching the race. The next, I was being pushed off the bleachers."

"You weren't pushed," a man standing nearby said. "The crowd just got a little carried away, that's all."

"Are you guys okay?" Chet asked, rushing through the small group of people who were surrounding the Hardys.

"Yeah," Joe said. "Sure."

"What happened with the race?" Frank asked, standing up.

Chet took a quick picture of Frank and Joe. "You mean you didn't see it?" he asked.

"It was so close, right down to the finish line." Then Chet's face fell. "But Mad Dog won. Sean came in second. He took the silver medal."

"That's too bad," Joe said.

"Look," Chet said, pointing to the field.

The medals ceremony was about to begin. The three marathon winners marched along a red carpet onto the field and then took their places on a three-tiered podium. Mad Dog stood on the highest level, leaning forward as an Olympic official placed a gold medal around his neck. Then Sean did the same, receiving his silver medal. Chet poked Joe in the ribs, beaming with pride. A Nigerian runner had taken the bronze. Then the French national anthem began to play over the P.A. system to honor Maddox Pomereau,

71

and at the same time the French, Irish, and Nigerian flags were raised in tribute to the winners.

Joe looked at the three winners and shook his head. "We're looking at three dead men," he whispered to Frank, "if we don't get busy."

Frank nodded silently. "We need a good lead, and quick."

"I'm going down there to get some more pictures," Chet said. He'd been popping one shot after another and hadn't heard Frank and Joe. "I promised everyone I'd get a picture of Sean on the winner's stand. You guys coming?"

"I think we'll just meet you for dinner," Frank said. "Now that the race is over, we've got to work fast."

"Where to?" Joe said once Chet had taken off.

"To the broadcast center," Frank said.

"The TV studios? Why?" Joe asked as they left the stadium. "Is there a clue I missed?"

"Let's say we got pushed," Frank said.

"Okay, we got pushed. So what?"

"Why did we get pushed just as the marathon race was ending?" Before Joe could answer, Frank went on. "Maybe someone didn't want us to see the end of the race. That's why I want to go to the TV studios. We can get a tape of the race and see what we missed."

"It's a long shot," Joe said, "but it's also the only shot we've got."

At the broadcast center, Frank had to show his

orange security credentials to three different people. Fifteen minutes later, though, he and Joe had permission to see the tapes. They were led into one of the editing suites, where a technician sat surrounded by a dozen large videotape recorders, monitors, and a control panel. The video engineer was a thin, nervous man with his hair slicked straight back.

"Vinnie Perlman," he said, the words racing out of his mouth. His hand darted out for a quick handshake and then snapped back. "What can I do for you?"

"We want to see tapes of the marathon finish," Frank said. He explained that they were working for Olympic security and were investigating the threats.

Vinnie's eyebrows shot up as he gave the Hardys a quick once-over, then he pointed to a couple of large, soft-cushioned chairs on casters. "Have a seat," he said. "I'll show you all five camera angles." He pressed buttons and hit the computer screen so fast his hands were almost a blur.

A few seconds later, the finish of the race appeared on five different TV monitors. Frank's eyes went from one screen to another, watching Mad Dog carefully, looking for something that didn't look right. "See anything strange?" he asked Joe.

Before Joe could answer, a voice behind them said, "Hi, guys."

Frank turned to see Cory Conner walking into the editing room.

"Wow," Conner said, looking straight at Joe's bruised eye. "You've got quite a rainbow there." He laughed and went on. "So you heard about my brother? He aced the pole vault at just under nineteen feet. I'd say he's only a few hours away from sweeping the gold."

"That's incredible," Frank said.

"Yeah," Cory said, "even though I tried not to, I got all choked up on the air. I didn't look stupid, did I, Vinnie?"

"Hey, I got choked up, too," Vinnie said, chewing his gum twice as fast.

Cory seemed to be getting choked up again. "My brother, the history maker. So what are you guys up to?"

"We're watching the marathon," Joe said.

"Yeah, that crazy Mad Dog pulled off another one," Cory said.

"Looks like he did it fair and square," Frank said.

Cory looked confused for a moment. "Yeah, why not? What do you mean?"

"They're working for Olympic security," Vinnie said with a quick jerk of his head in Frank and Joe's direction. "Trying to find out who sent those threatening notes."

"You mean, you're like undercover cops?" Cory asked.

Joe rolled his eyes at Vinnie. "Hey, Vinnie,

we're trying to keep that quiet, you know what I mean?" Joe said.

"Oh, sorry," Vinnie said.

"Don't worry," Cory said. "I won't tell anyone. In fact, I never would have guessed. I thought you were just trying to help your friend, the marathon runner. Do you have any leads?"

Joe hesitated. "Well, Mad Dog was our number-one suspect. That's why we wanted to check out the tape—to see if he was trying to pull anything sneaky or see if anyone made a move on the runners during the race."

"I didn't see anything," Vinnie said.

"Me, neither," Frank said.

"Hey, I've got a great idea. Can I do an interview with you guys?" Cory said.

Joe almost laughed, and he thought Frank looked as if someone had just stepped on his foot. Conner may know sports, Joe thought, but he doesn't know the first thing about detective work.

"Uh, maybe after we solve the case," Frank said, trying to be polite.

"Oh, yeah, right," Cory said, rolling his eyes. "I'd blow your cover, wouldn't I? Guess I'd make a terrible detective. Well, I've got to get my makeup checked." He headed for the door, but stopped and turned around. "Listen, if I can help you guys, just say the word. But you've got to promise me I get an exclusive first interview after you crack the case."

"It's a deal," Joe called as Cory left.

Frank turned back to the TV monitors. They were showing an interview with Mad Dog, who was surrounded by reporters.

"How do you feel, Mad Dog?" asked a reporter.

The runner smiled from ear to ear. "Terrific. Now I've proven to the world that I am what I said I was—the world's greatest marathon runner."

"Humble to the end," Joe said to Frank.

"What do you think of Sean O'Malley?" asked a reporter. "He gave you some stiff competition right down to the finish line."

"He came in second," Mad Dog said, "so you figure out what I think about him."

"What do you think about the threat to kill the marathoners, Mad Dog?" a reporter called out. "You'll be first in line if it happens."

A look of worry flashed over Mad Dog's face. "Interview's over," he said, and to make his point, he pushed his way through the crowd.

"Did you see that look?" Frank said, turning to Joe.

"Yeah, but what kind of clue was that?" Joe asked.

"One to file away for right now," Frank replied.

Before the Hardys left the TV studios, Frank asked for a sheet of paper and wrote down the finishing order of the marathon runners. Then they headed back to their hotel. As they walked through Sports City, Joe could see that security was getting tighter and tenser. The number of FBI guys lurking around in gray suits had doubled in the past twenty-four hours.

"I'm going to stop in and talk to Cathleen Barton," Joe said as they neared her office building. "See if they've got any new leads."

"Okay," Frank said. "But be sure to get out of there in time to meet us for Sean's celebration dinner."

"Right," Joe said. "Where are we meeting?"

"Chet said the name of the place is Scaldino's," Frank answered. "See you there at six."

At the restaurant that night Joe tried to keep Sean talking about the race and not about the murder threats. For a while it worked. Sean gave a mile-by-mile account of what it was like to run a marathon. Throughout the night Chet took snapshots of the celebration.

But eventually the subject everyone was avoiding came up.

"So did you guys find out who's going to come after me?" Sean asked, trying to sound casual.

"Well, not exactly," Joe said. "I talked to Cathleen Barton and the Olympic security people. The FBI is still thinking it's international terrorists."

"You don't think they're right, do you?" Sean asked.

Joe shook his head.

"We've got three good suspects we're following up on," Frank said seriously. "For one, there's Sigrid. You said yourself that she's got a gripe against the Olympic Committee, and she seemed pretty hostile. She might be the one who dumped chlorine in the pool. Or it could have been someone posing as a swimmer."

"Who else?" Sean said, frowning.

"Well, there's a boxer who's got a grudge against the whole world," Joe said, touching his black eye. "He's threatened to make everyone 'pay for it' if he doesn't get to box."

"And, of course, there's Mad Dog," Frank said. "If nothing happens to any of the runners, he climbs to the top of the list."

Sean's eyes almost sparkled when he heard that. "Really? Why?"

"Because if Mad Dog sent the notes just to make the other marathoners nervous, or get them to drop out," Frank explained, "then he got what he wanted. With his competition nervous, Mad Dog had a real edge."

"Hey," Chet said, "if you guys could prove that, Mad Dog would be disqualified for sure and Sean would win the gold medal. That would be fantastic!"

"Not so fast, cuz," Sean said. "It would be a beautiful thing to see Mad Dog get what was coming to him at last. But here's the honest truth:

I ran my best race and he still won. I'll always know that."

The waitress brought the food—steaks for everyone. Sean, Frank, and Joe picked up their knives and forks and started eating.

"Hey, hold it," Chet said, waving for them to stop. "I've got to get a shot of this food. The official Olympic marathon victory dinner."

"Don't forget to take a picture of the official Olympic salt-and-pepper shakers," Joe quipped.

"And what about the official Olympic sugar bowl," Frank added.

Chet took a picture of the Hardys holding up the items, and everyone laughed. They all decided it was a victory dinner and that it was time to start having fun. During the rest of the meal, no one mentioned the threats again.

After dinner, the four friends went back to Sean's dormitory, a large building with twenty rooms on each of the eight floors. In Sean's room there was one bed with rumpled sheets and one that hadn't been slept in—Bryan Dorset's bed.

"Hey, what's that?" Chet said excitedly, moving to a desk at the far end of the room.

On the desk next to Sean's bed was a large round layer cake covered in silver icing. It was decorated with shamrocks and Olympic emblems.

"Wow!" Chet pulled out his camera and took a picture. "What a cake!"

"Yeah," Joe said, looking around for a card or note, "but who's it from?"

"It must be from my coach," Sean said, a smile breaking across his face. "He's always doing things like this."

"Are you sure?" Frank said, hesitating.

"Definitely," Sean answered. "He sent me a cake after I won the Irish National Marathon last year."

"Okay, I guess," Frank said.

"Let's dig in," Chet said. "Your coach even left plates, forks, and a knife." He handed the long kitchen knife to Sean, saying, "I'll take an Olympic-size piece."

Sean cut slices of cake for everyone, and they began to eat. Joe dug into his slice of cake, but he was too full to eat very quickly. He and Frank talked to Sean, trying to keep his mind off the threats.

When they had all eaten big slices of cake, Joe wanted to go back to his own hotel room and go to bed.

"I'm bushed," he said. Suddenly, he was very sleepy.

A noise brought Joe's mind snapping back into focus. It was Chet, standing up and holding his plate carelessly so that his second piece of cake slid off onto the floor. Swaying on his feet, Chet moaned and held his stomach. His face had turned red, and he looked panicked.

"He's choking," Joe said, jumping up to help his friend.

But Chet crumpled heavily to the floor before Joe could get to him. And then, with a groan, Sean grabbed his stomach and fell over, too.

"Call nine-one-one!" Joe shouted. But all of a sudden his own stomach felt as if someone was twisting it like a wet towel. His feet felt heavy, and his head was dizzy.

"Frank, the cake," Joe managed to choke out before he keeled over onto a bed. "It was poisoned!"

9 Frank Smells
   a Rat

Frank couldn't get his eyes to open. When he finally did blink awake, everything in the room was out of focus. And there was an awful burning pain in his stomach.

He tried moving his arm, but somehow he couldn't get his muscles to cooperate. When he tried to sit up, Frank realized that he'd gotten tangled up in the phone cord. He remembered the last thing he'd been doing before he passed out. He'd tried to call for help. He must have gotten caught in the cord.

Except . . . he wasn't tangled at all. Someone had wrapped the cord around Frank's neck! More than once.

Frantically, he untangled the cord and at the

same time looked around the room in horror. Joe, Sean, and Chet were sprawled out on the carpet —and they weren't moving.

Frank sprang to his brother and tried to wake him up. "Joe. Joe!" he cried desperately.

At first, Joe didn't move. Frank shook him as hard as he could, and finally Joe started to moan.

"The cake," Joe said, speaking in a croaky voice.

By now Chet and Sean were also coming to. "What happened?" Chet groaned. "I think I'm going to be sick."

"Take some deep breaths," Frank said. "It'll pass."

"Frank, the cake," Joe said.

"I *know*. You already said that."

"That's not what I mean," Joe said. "It's gone!"

Frank's eyes darted to the desk—no cake, no box, no plates or forks, not even a crumb.

"It's okay," Frank said, trying to keep calm. Obviously a lot had gone on in the past few minutes. He and Joe needed some time to piece it together.

Joe stood up, holding on to the desk for balance. He was still unsteady on his feet. "Someone laced a cake with knockout drops and left it here," Joe said. "When we passed out, he—or she—came in and took the cake away."

"That's not all," Frank said. He'd already checked his back pocket. He knew Joe wasn't going to like the next piece of bad news. "They took our wallets and our Olympic IDs."

Joe felt for his wallet. It was gone. "What are we going to do now?" he asked, about to lose his temper.

"Calm down," Frank said. "We can get new ID cards from Cathleen Barton. Let's stick to the case. I figure whoever did it was watching us. He knew when we came back to the room, knew how long to wait before we'd be out cold."

"How long have we been out?" Sean asked.

Frank checked his watch. It was eleven-thirty. "We've been unconscious for about twenty minutes, I'd say," Frank answered.

"But how'd they get into my room?" Sean asked.

"Probably used the old credit card trick," Joe replied. "I'd show you—but our wallets are gone. Come on, Frank. Maybe the trail's still warm."

"Good idea," Frank agreed. "Will you guys be okay?"

Chet and Sean nodded glumly. Frank and Joe didn't waste any more time. They ran out of the room and into the dormitory lobby, asking each person they passed whether they'd seen anyone carrying a white bakery box. Finally, in the lounge, they found a man who had seen someone walk by with a box.

"What did he look like?" Joe asked the guy, who was dressed in sweats.

"Blond, good-looking, an athlete, I'd say. I didn't really notice."

"Okay. Which way did he go?"

"That way," the guy said, pointing to a door in the corner marked Exit.

Frank and Joe opened the door and went through. The door clicked shut behind them. They were in an alleyway behind the dormitory. There was a huge garbage dumpster and a long row of smaller garbage cans and recycling bins as well.

"Hey, look at that," Joe said.

One of the garbage cans was open, and there were mice crawling in and out of it. Frank moved toward the can, clapping his hands to scare away the mice.

Joe was right next to him. "Sorry, fellows. The party's over," he said, watching the mice scurry away.

In the moonlight Frank and Joe could see a few mice and a rat lying dead or unconscious beside the open bakery box. Inside was a round, half-eaten cake with silver icing.

"We're on the right trail," Joe said. "You better take the cake as evidence. I'm going on ahead to see where this alley leads. Maybe I can catch up with the guy."

Frank took a deep breath, then leaned into the garbage can and picked up the cake. He had to shake the edge of the box to dislodge a dead rat stuck in the icing.

"What's going on?" growled an angry voice.

Frank turned around and stared directly into a blinding light. But when the light moved, he could see a security guard. The guard had a misshapen, mashed face that looked as though it had been used as a kicking tee for a couple of seasons. He was frowning at Frank.

"Drop whatever you've got there," the guard said, reaching toward his holster.

"It's just a cake," Frank said.

The guard shined his light on the cake and then back into Frank's eyes again. "What's going on?" the guard demanded again.

"I'm working for Olympic security," Frank said.

"Oh, really?" the guard said with a laugh. "Then let's see your security credentials."

Frank gulped. "I don't have them. They were stolen."

"Yeah, right. So you're wandering around Sports City with no ID?" the guard said, backing away but keeping his flashlight in Frank's eyes.

"Look," Frank said, "I'm working for Cathleen Barton. You can call her and she'll tell you, if you don't believe me."

The guard laughed again. "I'm not stupid enough to call my boss in the middle of the night because some kid told me to. Just put the cake back where it belongs and get out of here before I arrest you."

Frank looked down at the cake, the only evidence they had. "I need this cake," he said.

The guard raised his hand to the holster on his waist. "Tough cookies. I'm giving you five to scram. One . . . two . . ."

Frank didn't wait for the guard to finish. Instead, he headed back to the front entrance of the dorm. There, security called Sean down to sign Frank in. Chet appeared in the lobby with Sean, and Frank explained that Joe was still searching outside for the culprit. The three friends sat on the empty lobby sofas arranged around a television to wait for Joe. The TV set was playing an Olympic wrap-up with the sound off. Sean watched himself come in second in the marathon again. Everyone felt more and more let down.

"What are we going to do now?" Frank said. "The case is falling apart. We haven't been able to nail down any of the suspects, and now we can't even trace the cake."

"Oh, yes we can," Chet said.

"We can?" Frank's face brightened.

"Sure," Chet said. "Who do we know who took *great* photos of that cake? Who do we know who'll get the film developed tomorrow and take the pictures around to bakeries to see if it's their cake?"

"Chet!" Frank cried out.

"I think the word you're looking for is genius," Chet said with a laugh.

87

"Close enough," Frank said, leaning over to slap him on the back.

"Frank," Sean said, "while we're taking a little break in the action maybe you can answer a question for me. Why am I still alive?"

"I've been thinking about that, too," Frank said. "Someone had a chance to kill you, but they only used knockout drops on you instead." Frank slumped down again in a chair. He felt tired, and nothing was making sense. "I don't know, Sean. Maybe it's all some kind of crazy joke. I wonder if Joe's found out anything."

Joe was standing in front of the pool building, the only place with lights on at the end of the trail he had followed. He hadn't seen anyone on the path leading out of the alley, but if the maniac who had stolen the cake had come this way, the swimming facility was the only place to hide.

Joe walked toward the door but froze before he got there. Standing inside were two Olympic security guards and two guys in gray suits—FBI for sure, Joe thought. Without his ID, Joe knew there was no way to get inside.

He dropped back and hid behind some bushes to the right of the doorway. It was as good a place as any to think of plan B.

When Joe had been there only about a minute, the doors opened. The men in gray suits and the two security guards stepped out and shook hands. Then the FBI agents left and the guards went to check around the outside of the building.

As soon as they were gone, Joe leaped out of the bushes and headed for the doors. What were the chances they were open? He yanked on one handle. Locked. Then he tried another. Locked. There were six doors all together. Finally, on the fifth try, the door opened.

Joe smiled at his good luck and slipped inside as fast as he could.

As he neared the pool, Joe heard a loud splash—the sound of a body diving into water and swimming. He followed the sound and found a lone swimmer climbing out of the pool. It was Sigrid Randers-Perhson, the swimmer who had a grudge against the Olympic Committee. Her short blond hair was wet and loose. And she was wearing a tank-style bathing suit— navy blue with a red stripe! The swimmer Joe had been looking for had been wearing a blue and red suit and a white T-shirt. If Sigrid put on a T-shirt over her suit, she would fit the description.

There was a splash. Sigrid dove in again and started swimming laps.

Joe walked toward the edge of the pool to meet her. "Nice stroke," he called. His voice echoed off the three-story-high tile walls.

Sigrid swam to the side of the pool and pulled herself out, shooting him a nervous look at first. "I know you, don't I?" she said.

"Yeah," Joe said. "I'm a friend of Sean O'Malley. I saw you at lunch the other day."

She nodded. "Sean ran a good race," she said.

Joe sat down on a bench and tossed her the large towel that lay next to him. "Yeah," he said. "What about you?"

"I plan to teach people a few lessons about Sigrid Randers-Perhson," she said, toweling her hair.

Maybe it was just her way of being confident. Or maybe it was her awkwardness with English. But Joe thought she sounded angry again—and he thought her words sounded like another threat.

"How long have you been here?" he asked.

She moved to the bench, sat down several feet away from him, and put on her sneakers. "Why do you want to know?" she said coldly.

"I meant, how much do you practice at night?"

"Oh. At least two hours," Sigrid said. "I've been here since ten. I'm going back to the dorm now," she said, standing up. "Good night, Mr.—?"

Joe stood, too, and extended his hand. "Joe Hardy," he said, shaking her hand. But then Joe looked down at her fingers, still resting in his hand. Her skin was wrinkled like a prune. She'd been in the water a long time—far too long to be the person he was looking for.

"Well, good night," Joe said. "Good luck in your meets."

Since he'd reached another dead end, Joe decided to head back to the dorms, too. Outside the natatorium, even at midnight, Joe was surprised by the activity in Sports City. There were trucks bringing in food and maintenance crews cleaning the grounds. Joe also saw security forces crisscrossing each other on their patrols.

In the distance Joe saw the Olympic flame. Overhead, there was the unmistakable darting pattern of bats in flight. An owl screeched, and Joe almost jumped.

Then, all at once, as Joe stopped under the white light of a mercury street lamp, he saw something coming toward him. Something running . . . low to the ground . . . gaining speed on all fours.

Before Joe could even decide which way to run, a vicious dog leaped at him, growling and snarling, baring its teeth as it lunged for Joe's neck.

10 Midnight Attack

Joe lay motionless on the ground. Panicked, he watched the dog circle him. It woofed and growled in a deep husky voice. The dog was enormous—a white Great Dane with black splotches on its coat.

His heart thumping, Joe put his arms up to protect his face and started to get to his feet. But the movement triggered the dog. It attacked, pouncing on Joe's leg with a vicious snarl.

Joe heard a terrible ripping sound as the dog's teeth tore into the leg of his jeans. The dog pulled and jerked until he tore away part of Joe's pants leg.

"Emperor, get off!" a voice called, running toward Joe.

Suddenly the dog yelped as it was jerked back by its studded leather collar. Joe struggled to sit up. He saw someone holding back the dog. It was Vinnie Perlman, the video editor from the TV studio.

"Vinnie?" Joe said, gasping for breath.

"Joe?" Vinnie asked back. "Wow. Sorry. I didn't think anyone was around or I never would have let him off the leash."

"That's okay," Joe said, getting to his feet shakily.

Vinnie clamped a chain leash on the dog's collar. "This here's Emperor. He's a harlequin Great Dane—the only dog I know that's been kicked out of obedience school." Vinnie tried to keep the dog away from Joe, but it was obvious he couldn't control him. "What are you doing out so late, kid?"

"I thought I was following a lead on our case," Joe said. "But it didn't work out." Joe had an idea. "Listen, Vinnie," he said. "Could my brother and I come by tomorrow and look at some more tapes? It would be great if we could see what you have on Kyung Chin's accident. Interviews after the fall, stuff like that. Check out if we can spot anything suspicious on the tape of the accident."

Vinnie's mouth twitched and he looked away. "I'll tell you, if it was up to me, I'd say you and your brother are good kids. I like what you're doing and I'd show you tapes."

"That sounds like a no," Joe said.

Vinnie still wouldn't look at Joe. "What I'm saying is that I got orders that you two are no longer welcome persons in my editing suite."

"You're kidding," Joe said with surprise. "Why?"

"I said I got *orders*, not an explanation. But I'll tell you this—if the orders came from any higher, they'd be carved on stone tablets. I'm real sorry, but what can I do?"

Joe frowned. "But we've got security clearance."

"Sorry," Vinnie said. "Gotta go. Actually, the dog's gotta go and I gotta keep up with him. Good luck, kid."

When Joe got back to the hotel room, the lights were still on. But Frank was asleep in his clothes on one bed. Sean was sleeping on the other bed, and Chet was on the couch.

Joe took his shoes off quietly and set them down on the soft carpet.

"Joe? Are you okay?" Frank whispered. "Where've you been?"

"I stopped to feed a dog," Joe said, yawning and sitting on the edge of the bed. He showed his brother the torn leg of his jeans.

Frank whistled softly when he saw the pants. Then he got a can of soda out of a small refrigerator in the kitchenette in an alcove at one end of the room. Frank took a swig, then passed the can to Joe, who'd joined him. As they shared the soda, they exchanged information. Joe told his brother about seeing Sigrid in the pool and about running into Vinnie and his dog. Frank had news, too—about losing the cake because of the security guard.

"We also saw Mad Dog in the lobby tonight," Frank said.

Joe's eyebrows shot up. "And?"

"And I asked him where he'd been all night. He said he was having dinner with hotshots from a running-shoe company between eight and eleven. Says he never left their sight."

"Sounds like an airtight alibi," Joe said. "If he's telling the truth, he couldn't have given us the cake."

"He's telling the truth. I called Cathleen Barton, and she had the FBI confirm Mad Dog's story," Frank said. "She also told me that there hasn't been a single attempt on Mad Dog's life."

Joe held the cold soda can to his forehead. "This case gets weirder and weirder," he said.

"Want to play a game?" Frank asked.

"Like what?" Joe said with a yawn.

"Let's take turns being suspects and see if we can figure this thing out," Frank said. "I'll be Mad Dog. Let's say I sent a note to the marathon runners saying I'd kill them, because I want to scare everyone. It gives me an edge. And it worked. I won the race. Prove that I did it."

"Well, for starters, I know you did it because nothing happened to you," Joe said.

"But I won the race," Frank said. "I don't have to make good on my threat now, do I?"

"No, you don't," Joe replied, realizing Frank's point. "But someone tried to poison Sean with that cake. If Mad Dog was at dinner and he doesn't really have a motive . . . Hey, I don't think you're a viable suspect anymore."

"I think you're right," Frank said. "Now who do you want to be?"

"Okay," Joe said. He boosted himself onto the kitchen counter and stretched his legs out. "I'm the no-name suspect. Blond hair, blue bikini bathing suit, athletic. I put the cake in Sean's room. What do you know about me?"

Frank sat on the opposite counter. "You can't count and you're not good at your job," Frank said, smiling.

"Huh?"

"You started with the marathoner who came in second place—not first. And you only drugged him, you didn't kill him. If you want to kill all the marathon runners, you'd better put it in high gear, because the Olympics are almost over."

"What else?" Joe asked.

Frank was silent. For a moment, only Chet's snoring in the other room broke the silence.

"You weren't making a real death threat," Frank said finally. "It was just a joke, or a trick. You're after something else, but I don't know what. But I *do* know this about you."

"What?" Joe asked.

"You can get in and out of the athlete's dorm with no trouble," Frank answered. "And get close enough to the Olympic flame, the gym equipment, and the pool to sabotage them. I'll bet you have an Olympic ID card."

"Yeah, right," Joe said. "So I'm an athlete, or a coach, or someone who works for the Olympics, maybe even an Olympic official."

Frank went over to the desk and picked up a sheet of paper, then walked back to the kitchenette. "This is the list of marathon winners that I wrote down at the TV studio," he said, reading it over quickly. "Any one of them had a motive *before* the marathon. But not one of them has a motive after the race."

"Okay, then, maybe it's not a marathoner. Maybe it's an athlete from a totally different event," Joe said. "What about Chili Pepper?"

Frank was staring closely at the list, holding the paper up to the light. He didn't seem to be listening to Joe.

"Give up on the list of marathoners," Joe said. "It's a dead end."

"Uh-uh," Frank said, shaking his head from side to side. "Just the opposite, unless I'm wrong. Look at this piece of paper."

Joe took the paper and gave Frank a quizzical look. Then Frank pulled another sheet of paper from his pocket and handed it to his brother. Joe read the second sheet. It was the death threat Sean had received. "What am I supposed to be looking for?" Joe asked.

"I'll make it easy for you," Frank said, taking both sheets and holding them side by side up to the light. "Look at the watermarks."

Joe looked down and saw that the watermark—a pattern pressed into each sheet of paper—was the same on both sheets. It read Peterman's Papers and had the logo of the Peterman Company.

"It's the same paper," Joe said. "So what? I mean, lots of people use it. Dad even uses Peterman's bond to type up his reports, doesn't he?"

"Maybe," Frank said. "But I still think it's a clue. There are lots of other paper companies. What are the chances that the threatening note would come on the same kind of paper that the TV network uses?"

"Okay, let's say you're right," Joe said. "Where does that get us? You're saying the threat came from someone at the broadcast center?"

Frank nodded. "It's a possibility."

"Well, that would explain one thing I found out tonight," Joe said. "Vinnie told me that we are no longer welcome to screen any more tapes— which means that someone over there doesn't want us snooping around. But why would someone in broadcasting want to sabotage the Olympics?"

Frank raised an eyebrow. "A death threat is an exciting story," he said. "Big ratings. That's what television is all about. It might even be Cory Conner. He's the one who reported the threat in the first place."

Joe thought for a moment. "I don't think so," he said. "I mean, whoever sent the death threats also poured oil in the Olympic torch and chlorine in the pool. I can't believe someone in broadcasting would do all that just to get an exciting story. Not even Cory Conner," Joe added.

"Maybe we should call Cathleen Barton and show her the watermarks on the paper," Frank suggested. "See what the FBI has to say about it."

The phone rang before Joe could respond to his brother. Joe got up and grabbed the phone near his bed on the third ring. "Hello?" he said.

"Who is this?" asked a man's voice on the other end.

"Joe Hardy. Who is this?"

"Listen carefully," the voice demanded.

"I'm listening to every word you say," Joe answered.

"If you want information about the death threats, go to the boat rental house at the south end of the Tuscarawas River. Tomorrow afternoon at two o'clock."

"Who is this?" Joe asked again. "Why don't you tell me what you know right now?"

"Don't argue," the man said. "Because if you don't come, there's no way you can save Sean O'Malley's life." And with that, the line went dead.

11 The Waiting Game

"Hey," Joe cried, holding the receiver away from his ear.

"Who was that?" Frank asked, coming into the room.

"I wish I knew!"

"Was it a threat?" Frank asked, keeping his voice low so he wouldn't wake the others.

"Actually," Joe said, replacing the receiver, "whoever that was wants us to meet him at the south end of the Tuscarawas River tomorrow. He said he has information about the death threats and he'll give it to us there—and only there."

Frank thought for a moment. "In other words, he either wants to get us out of the way or get us someplace where we're totally vulnerable. Does he think we're amateurs? It's a setup."

Joe nodded. "Yeah, but the only problem is, there's a prize if we go. Sean gets to live. The caller said we don't have a chance of saving him if we don't show."

"Then we don't have any choice," Frank said grimly.

First thing the next morning, the Hardys went straight to the Olympic security offices. Cathleen Barton sat behind a desk piled with paperwork. The look on her face was just a little more serious than the day before. Frank could see that the case was getting to her.

"What's up?" she asked.

"A lot," Joe said, sitting down opposite her desk. "We got a call late last night from someone who says he has information about who's making the Olympic threats. He wants us to meet him this afternoon at the Tuscarawas River."

Cathleen was silent. "Is he ratting on the guy we're after or is he the guy himself?" she wondered out loud.

"Don't know," Joe said. "Frank doesn't think he'll show. He thinks it's just a trick to get us out of the picture at the right moment."

"That's possible, but let's think positive," Cathleen said. She reached for her phone. "I'd better get the FBI in on this." She made the call and set up an appointment for Frank and Joe to meet with the agents in charge of the case.

When she hung up the phone, Joe asked, "You don't happen to have a couple spare Olympic ID cards around, do you?"

"What happened to the ones I gave you?" Cathleen asked. "Get tired of them?"

"Someone knocked us out last night and grabbed them," Frank explained.

Cathleen leaned forward on her elbows as Frank and Joe filled her in on the poisoned cake and what they had found out afterward about the various suspects. Unfortunately, it wasn't much.

Then Cathleen shared her latest information. A man had walked into a police station last night with a guilty conscience, she said. He turned himself in for the hit-and-run accident. The FBI checked his story out, and it turned out to be true. He was the drunk driver who had run into Bryan Dorset.

"So his accident was really just an accident," Joe said. "It wasn't part of the Olympic threats."

"Right," Cathleen said. "Oh—and I meant to tell you. The hospital says that Bryan is going to be okay eventually, although it will take time. He may even be able to run again."

Frank smiled and then moved on to another subject. "I've got a clue for you—for what it's worth. The watermark on the note sent to Sean is identical to the mark on a piece of paper I picked up at the broadcast center."

"Yeah, we know," Cathleen said. At Frank's surprised look, she went on. "The FBI lab boys confirmed that the first note, which was sent to the Olympic Committee, was on the same paper used by the television network," Cathleen said. "But that doesn't mean that it necessarily came from the broadcast center. Can you guys think of anyone over there with a motive?"

Frank looked at Joe. "Cory Conner?" he said. He was fishing, but Cory and Vinnie were the only people he knew there. "He deliberately leaked stories about trouble at the Olympics. But he wouldn't tell us his sources."

Cathleen shook her head. "You're going to have to come up with harder evidence than that. Asking the FBI to point a finger at Cory Conner would be a very unpopular move."

"The FBI sure keeps ahead of the game," Joe said.

"They're probably having tomorrow night's dinner right now," Cathleen said with a laugh.

Later that morning, the Hardys met with the FBI agent in charge, a man named McCracken. He was a heavyset man in his forties, wearing a dark blue suit, a dark tie, and a weary look. He gave them new ID cards and then told them the plan.

The Hardys were going to borrow a small white car—one of the official Olympic security vehicles—and drive to the river. At two o'clock they would be in the parking lot, waiting for the mysterious caller to show up. FBI agents would be hiding nearby.

Joe drove to where the Tuscarawas River cut a path a hundred yards wide down through forested hills. He pulled the car into a gravel parking lot at ten minutes before two, as instructed.

As soon as the Hardys got out of their car they saw joggers, swimmers, and kyackers walking through the parking lot. All were heading for the river. But Frank and Joe already knew that some of those people were really FBI agents in disguise.

Frank sat on the hood of the car, trying to look as inconspicuous as possible. Joe paced nearby. They waited. Twenty minutes, thirty minutes went by. They watched people coming and going. Three o'clock. Now both Hardys sat on the car's hood. Was this guy ever going to show up?

At three-thirty, a neon-painted van pulled up and parked right next to Frank and Joe. Frank went on alert, until he saw Agent McCracken climbing out of the back. Then he and Joe eased off the hood of the car, looking disappointed.

"Sorry, guys," Agent McCracken said. "I'm declaring this a no-show." He craned his neck and spoke into a small microphone concealed behind his lapel. "It's a no-show. Fold the tents."

As invisibly as they came, the FBI agents started to leave. Engines roared to life and cars pulled out of the parking lot.

McCracken turned back to Frank. "It was a good try, just too good to be true," he said. "See ya around, guys. Stay out of trouble."

"Yeah," Frank said after the agent had moved on. "Now what?"

"Lunch," Joe said. "I haven't eaten since breakfast, and I'm starved."

Frank smiled, but the truth was he only felt like eating when things were going their way. And the way this case was going, he might not be hungry for weeks.

They got back on the highway and drove a few minutes until they came to a little log cabin restaurant with a freshly painted sign that said "Olympic Diner. We Feed Olympic-Size Appetites."

"That's the place for me," Joe said. Spinning into the gravel parking lot, he brought the car to a quick stop. Frank practically had to run to keep up with his brother going into the restaurant. Joe headed straight for the long wooden counter and climbed up on a stool.

Frank opened a menu, but Joe wasn't waiting.

"Pancakes," he called to the waitress. "And make that a double stack."

Frank ordered a hamburger and fries. While they waited for their lunch, the Hardys went over what they knew.

106

"I'll bet the guy saw all the agents and decided not to take a chance," Joe said.

"Either that," Frank said, "or the whole thing was a setup."

Their food came, and Frank and Joe ate silently. Neither of them felt very hopeful about the case.

"That was our best lead," Joe said after he mopped up the last of the maple syrup on his plate.

"Don't I know it," Frank said. "Let's just hope nothing happened back at Sports City while we were gone."

They paid the check and left the restaurant. Once they were back in the car, Joe floored the gas pedal. Frank turned on the radio, scanning the stations for news—news that he didn't want to hear—about another tragedy at the Olympics. What would it be this time? They listened as Joe drove back into town on the flat two-lane country road.

"Nothing," Frank said, turning off the radio.

"No news is good news," Joe said.

Just then the engine coughed and sputtered, and the car coasted to a stop—right on a railroad crossing.

"Come on, Joe. Don't fool around. It's against the law to stop on the railroad tracks."

Joe turned the ignition and the engine whined unhappily. "I hate to tell you this," Joe said, "but it's *not* against the law to run out of gas."

Frank's eyes darted to the gas gauge. "You're kidding," he said. "We had a full tank this morning. Now it's empty?"

Joe slapped the wheel. "Someone must have drained the tank while we were in the restaurant."

Just then Joe heard a whistle and the sound of a train engine off in the distance.

"Joe!" Frank shouted, pointing to the left.

Joe saw the bright headlights of a train. The whistle blared again, louder this time.

Bells started clanging, and lights flashed as the arms of the crossing gate dropped across their path.

"We're trapped!" Frank yelled.

12 Killer Tracks

Joe's heart raced as he sat behind the wheel of the car, frantically turning the key in the ignition. The train horn was blasting a constant warning scream as it roared toward the crossing.

Frank ran around the car and yanked open the driver's door. "Forget it. That train's coming fast! Let's go!" The whistle sounded again, closer this time.

Joe was still turning the key in the ignition. "It's going to start," he said.

BRAAAAATT!

"Let's go!" Frank screamed again. Finally Joe popped his seat belt and jumped out of the car.

With only seconds left, Joe and Frank sprinted

across the train tracks. Frank was near the open end of the crossing gate. He edged around it.

But Joe didn't have time. He had to get over that gate—and there was only one way to do it.

In one smooth move, Joe jumped it like a hurdle, just before the train arrived.

"I did it!" Joe shouted, realizing that he had just cleared a hurdle for the first time in his life—and in perfect Olympic form.

At that same moment, there was an ear-shattering crash and the awful scrape of metal against metal. The speeding train had tried to stop, but it was going too fast. It roared over the little Olympic security car, crushing it, dragging it, and then pushing it off the track in a mangled heap.

When it was all over, Joe looked at his brother. "Don't say it. I know we should have bailed out a lot sooner. But I thought the car would start. Cathleen's going to kill us."

"It wasn't exactly our fault," Frank said. "We didn't drain the gas tank."

"Yeah," Joe said. "But who did?"

The Hardys had to stay at the scene of the accident for hours. First the police and then the FBI questioned them. Then the investigators questioned the conductor and all the witnesses. It wasn't until early that evening that Joe and Frank were finally driven in a patrol car back to Cathleen Barton's office. There, they explained the whole thing all over again to her, and apologized for destroying one of the security force's cars.

Finally, at about seven o'clock they hurried up to their hotel room, hungry and exhausted. They showered, called room service, and ordered almost one of everything on the menu. Then they sat down with Chet and Sean and told them about everything that had happened.

The food arrived on four carts piled with plates and silver covers to keep it warm. Sitting on couches and cushioned chairs, the four friends dug into their steaks and fries, shrimp cocktails, club sandwiches, fried zucchini, slices of pie, and bowls of fruit salad.

Joe and Frank did most of the talking, telling first about how no one showed up at the river, and then about the car getting smashed at the railroad crossing. Once they were done, Chet told the Hardys about the progress he'd made on the case. "I couldn't find a one-hour photo place," Chet explained. "So I just described the cake to everyone."

"Did you find out where it came from?"

"Yup," Chet said. "Lorber's Bakery. I talked to the owner, Liz Lorber. She remembered the cake, but not who bought it."

"Big help," Frank said.

"She did say one thing," Chet went on. "Those shamrocks on the cake? She didn't put them there."

"Bingo," Joe said. "That must be how he added the knockout drops."

"No wonder I felt a little *green*," Frank joked.

The whole time they had been talking, the television had been on in the background with the sound turned off. Now Joe noticed that the TV was showing highlights of Adam Conner sweeping every event of the decathlon and scoring a record-breaking 9,100 points.

Joe turned up the sound in time to hear the announcer describing Adam's perfect—and unexpected—high jump, as well as his brilliant performances in the hurdles, javelin, discus, and fifteen-hundred-meter race.

"I'm telling you," Joe said, working on a piece of apple pie, "I could win the decathlon . . . if someone would just win the hurdles for me."

"I know," Chet teased. "You told us that before and it didn't make any sense then, either."

"Why not?" Joe said. "It makes perfect sense to me."

"No, it doesn't," Chet argued. "You can't win the decathlon if you don't compete in all ten events. It's not called the pick-seven or the best-eight-of-ten. You've got to be able to do all ten events yourself."

Suddenly Frank jumped to his feet so fast he made Sean spill his cola. "Wait a minute! That's it!" Frank practically shouted.

"What?" Joe asked.

"What you just said. That you could win the decathlon if someone ran the hurdles for you. What if that's how Adam Conner won?"

"Huh?" Joe asked.

"What if Adam's twin brother stood in for him in some event?" Frank cried.

Joe, Chet, and Sean were stunned. But something told Joe that Frank had a point—a very good one.

"Wait a minute," Chet said. "Brilliant theory. I mean I can really see it. Twins always trade places with each other, right? But what does this have to do with the threats to the marathoners?"

Sean nodded. "That's exactly what I was going to ask."

"What if it was all a diversion?" Frank asked, thinking quickly. "The marathon was being run at the same time as the final day of the decathlon. What if the threat was a ploy to distract everyone during the decathlon, so they wouldn't notice the switch on the field?"

"But what about the fact that Cory was injured and he never competed athletically again?" Chet said.

"That's what he *said*," Frank answered. "But who knows if it's true?"

"You could be right," Joe said slowly.

"I *know* I'm right," Frank said. "I mean, look at Adam Conner's performance. It was practically superhuman! You just heard that announcer say that Adam wasn't expected to do well in the high jump, and instead he set a world's record. Can you explain that?"

"No, but—"

Frank interrupted his brother. "And look how well their plan worked! The whole world was watching the marathon. Even *we* didn't pay much attention to the decathlon, and we were right there in the stadium."

"You're right," Chet agreed.

"Look at it logically," Frank went on. "Nothing—absolutely nothing—has happened to any Olympic athlete since the marathon."

"True," Sean said. "But things have happened to you guys."

"I have a feeling I know why," Frank said. "Cory saw us the day we were at the broadcast center. He knew we were snooping around. Vinnie even told him we were working for Olympic security."

"What made you suspect Cory in the first place?" Chet asked.

"I *didn't* suspect him—until just now, when Joe said he'd need a stand-in to win the decathlon," Frank explained. "But I've always been bothered by certain things. Like the story that Adam Conner is ambidextrous. Everyone talks about how he changes his style for different events. Sometimes he takes off on his right foot, sometimes he uses his left."

"So what?" Chet asked.

114

"Nothing," Frank said. "But I kept asking myself why. Most athletes try to develop a consistent style. Do things the same way every time."

Joe nodded, thinking. "You figure that Adam's no different. Maybe he always uses his right foot. And maybe Cory always uses his left," Joe said.

"Exactly," Frank said.

"Okay, so what do we do now?" Joe asked.

"I say it's time to check out Cory Conner," Frank said.

"Fine, but we don't know where he's staying," Joe said.

"I do," Chet said. Everyone looked at Chet in surprise. "I saw him coming out of his hotel yesterday, so I ran over there and took a picture of him. He's right across the street."

"Chet!" Frank cried, "you're—"

"A genius," Sean said, slapping Chet's back.

Ten minutes later, Frank and Joe were crossing the street in front of their hotel, heading for the exclusive Park Tower. They went straight through the carpeted lobby to the house phones next to the marble registration desk.

Joe picked up the receiver, and an operator answered.

"Cory Conner's room, please," Joe said. He waited, crossing his fingers, hoping Cory wouldn't be in. The phone rang and rang.

"Good. He's not there," Joe reported to Frank as he hung up the phone. Then he picked it up again and this time asked for the hotel's housekeeping department. "Hello, housekeeping?" he said. "This is Cory Conner. I'm in the lobby and I'm going out for a while. Could you put some extra towels in my room right away, please? Thanks. You know my room number, correct?" Joe smiled at the voice on the other end, then said, "That's right, suite twelve thirty-six. Thanks."

"Nice work, Joe," Frank said, smiling.

A few minutes later Frank and Joe were standing in the hallway on the twelfth floor. They spotted a housekeeper going into Cory's room with an armful of towels.

"When she comes out," Joe said, "I'll get her attention and you slip into the suite behind her."

It only took a moment to make the plan work. When the housekeeper came out without the towels, Joe bumped into a decorative table that stood in the hallway near the suite. A large vase of dried flowers on the table nearly fell over. While the maid was looking suspiciously at Joe, Frank slipped into the room behind her back. Joe waited for her to leave, then crept back toward Cory Conner's door and knocked softly. Frank let him in.

"Come on in," Frank said.

Joe let out a low whistle as he took a quick glance around the living room. It was filled with leather couches and chairs, a large-screen projection TV, and a complete entertainment center. Then he saw that there was also a bedroom, bathroom, and small kitchenette. "This place is huge!" Joe said. "How much do you think it costs to stay here?"

"You'd probably have to choose between this and a four-year college education," Frank said.

They started searching in Cory's bedroom, which was a mess of dirty clothes, videotapes, and video gear.

"What are we looking for?" Joe asked, tossing aside a bathrobe and a pair of socks.

"Something that proves Cory's been training for one of the Olympic events," Frank said.

Suddenly Joe froze. "Frank," he whispered. "Listen."

From the living room, both Hardys heard the sound of a key in the doorknob. Someone was coming into the suite.

Joe motioned to Frank, and the two of them quickly squeezed into a closet, closing the door behind them.

Joe heard footsteps in the bedroom. He held his breath, letting it out as quietly as possible. Someone was in the bedroom now, opening and closing drawers and humming to himself. Joe heard the person taking off his shoes.

It *had* to be Cory. Was he going to open the closet? Joe's heart raced in his chest. He looked at Frank and saw his brother's eyes grow wide with fear. If they were caught now, the whole case would be blown.

Joe heard some more sounds of clothes being

117

removed. Finally, after a few minutes, Cory left the room. Joe heard the door open and then close with a click.

Cautiously, Frank and Joe stepped out of the closet and looked around. The only thing that was different was a new small pile of clothes on the freshly made bed. "He just dropped by to change," Joe said. "Good thing he never hangs his clothes up! I wonder where he's going now?"

"Swimming," Frank said.

"How do you know?" Joe was amazed.

"Because when he left, it sounded like he was wearing flip-flops."

"Frank—you're a genius," Joe said.

"Don't let Chet hear you say that," Frank joked.

"Come on," Joe said, heading for the door. "Let's find the pool. I think it's time we talked to Cory Conner."

They took an elevator up to the hotel's pool and spa center, a glass-enclosed structure on the roof. There were three separate areas—a lap pool, a sauna, and an exercise room—plus men's and women's locker rooms.

"Where do we look first?" Joe whispered, as they stepped out of the elevator.

"No problem. There he is," Frank said, motioning toward the small mirrored room on the right. Joe followed Frank's gaze, looking in through a solid glass wall to an exercise room

118

filled with workout equipment. Cory had his back to them and was pedaling an exercise bike.

Joe watched Cory's legs pumping and his arms moving on the bike, his blond hair blowing.

"Check it out," Frank said. "Cory Conner's got a blue bikini swimsuit with a red stripe!"

13 Seeing Double

Joe tugged at Frank's arm. "Come on," he said. "I think Cory's got some explaining to do."

"Hold on," Frank said, making a time-out sign with his hands. "All we've got are suspicions. We can't prove anything until we catch Cory and Adam making a mistake."

"Well, that's just great," Joe said, pounding his fist angrily. "The decathlon is over. They won't make any more mistakes."

Frank turned around and hit the elevator call button. "Maybe they made a mistake we didn't see," he said. "Come on. I need to find a phone."

They rode the elevator back down to the lobby, where Frank found a bank of pay phones. He picked up the receiver, got a number from information, dialed, and hoped for a miracle.

"Vinnie Perlman, please," Frank said when the receptionist answered at the broadcast center. Soon Vinnie's voice came on the line.

"Vinnie, it's Frank Hardy. Remember me? You showed some tapes to my brother and me."

"Yeah, yeah. You're the one without the black eye."

"Right," Frank said with a laugh. "Vinnie, we *need* to look at some more tapes."

"Sorry, Frank, but like I told your brother—no go. You must have been wearing cleats when you stepped on someone's toes around here. I got strict orders—the strictest—not to show you any tapes."

"I know," Frank said. "But Joe and I think we know who's behind all the trouble at the Olympics. We need to see some more tapes to prove it."

There was a long silence. "Okay, Frankie, I'm hooked," Vinnie said. "Reel me in. What's the scoop?"

"I can't tell you right now," Frank said, looking around to see if anyone was listening. "It's not safe."

"No sweat, Mr. Mystery," Vinnie said. "Be here at midnight."

"Great! Thanks, Vinnie," Frank said, and hung up the phone. He looked at his watch. It was eight o'clock. "In four hours we'll know whether we're heroes or bozos."

Frank and Joe tried to fill the next four hours with some of the fun they had missed during the week. They went with Chet and Sean to watch the basketball finals, the battle for the gold, from the front row. Then they stopped by the Track Meat, where most of the athletes were hanging out after their events had finished. Frank wondered whether they would run into Adam Conner there, but he was a no-show.

At about eleven-thirty that night, Sean and Chet walked with the Hardys through Sports City. Sean ran into some friends from Ireland who invited him to a dorm party, and Chet went along. Then the Hardys headed alone toward the broadcast center.

When they walked into the TV building, the receptionist handed over two visitor passes. "Vinnie says go right back," she said.

They walked quickly to the editing suite and found Vinnie waiting for them.

"Help yourself," Vinnie said, pointing to chairs and several leftover pizzas. "You know, someone could hang me out to dry for letting you guys in here. But to tell you the truth, I'm the kind of guy who sort of likes to break rules."

"Thanks, Vinnie," Frank said. "We really appreciate it. What we want to see are all the tapes of the decathlon. Plus anything else you've got on Adam Conner."

"And Cory Conner, too," Joe added.

A smile twitched hesitantly over Vinnie's face. "What are you two up to?"

"I'd rather not say until we have some evidence," Frank said. "Right now, we're just checking out a hunch."

"Just a couple of detectives nosing around," Vinnie said with a laugh. "Okay, keep me in suspense. Chew on some cold pizza while I dig up the tapes."

He was gone for a few minutes, loading tapes into machines in the room next door. Then they started watching the playback on the monitors in front of them.

There was a lot to watch—the whole two-day decathlon event, plus all the on-camera interviews and commentary from Cory Conner. The videos even included an interview Cory did with his brother before the games began.

Frank stared at the monitors, afraid to blink because he might miss the clue that would prove Cory substituted for his brother, Adam.

Suddenly, in the middle of an interview between Cory and one of the decathletes, Frank yelled, "Stop."

Joe paused the tape and looked at Frank. "What's up?" he asked.

"Cory's holding the microphone in his right hand," Frank explained.

Joe picked up on Frank's point. "He's been

123

completely left-handed in every other tape we've seen."

"Maybe his hand got tired," Vinnie said. "It happens."

Vinnie had a point, and Frank knew they needed more evidence. But at least they had a start.

"What event was going on at the time?" Frank asked.

"Gotta be the decathlon," Vinnie said, tapping both feet nervously. "That's the main thing they hired Cory to cover."

"It was the high jump," Joe said. "I heard the announcer. Let's see it."

Vinnie spun in his swivel chair toward his computer screen. "High jump—comin' right up," he said. His hands seemed to fly in all directions at once, hitting buttons and controls.

Vinnie played a tape of Adam getting ready to do his high jump, and Frank asked him to stop again.

"See? Adam started off on his left foot, but he's been consistently right-handed and right-footed in everything else," Joe said with a smile. "You know what I think? I think Adam's right-handed and Cory's left-handed. And I think this business about Adam being ambidextrous is a big whitewash."

"They must be what's called mirror-image twins," Vinnie said.

124

"What's that?" Frank asked.

"Twins who look exactly alike, except they're not really. If one of them has a mole on the left, the other one has it on the right. That sort of thing. They're mirror images of each other. Usually, one is left-handed and the other is a righty."

"Great!" Frank exclaimed. "Then that explains it."

"Explains what?" Vinnie asked.

"Let's look at the second day of the decathlon, and then we'll tell you."

Vinnie tapped his touch-sensitive screen and began showing different tapes of the next day's decathlon events. On the top row of monitors, Vinnie played tapes of Cory, the reporter. On the bottom row, he played tapes of Adam competing.

By the time they were done comparing all the tapes, Frank and Joe felt they had their proof. Adam was right-handed and right-footed in all the decathlon events, except two—the high jump and the pole vault. In those events, he started his run with his left foot. Meanwhile, Cory was left-handed in all his interviews and commentaries, except for two. The interviews that took place during the high jump and pole vault events showed a right-handed Cory Conner. If it really was Cory . . . The conclusion seemed obvious.

"We think Cory and Adam traded places, so that Cory could help his brother win the decathlon," Frank finally told Vinnie.

Vinnie let out a long whistle. "Even if that's true," he asked, "what's this got to do with the death threats?"

"We figure it was a diversion," Joe said, "to make sure everyone paid more attention to the marathon than to the decathlon events. That way, people wouldn't notice the switch."

Vinnie thought about it for a moment. "Sounds to me like you guys are about to make Olympic history by blowing the lid on this scam," Vinnie said.

"I don't know if we've got them for sure," Frank said. "But with these tapes, we've got enough to go to the Olympic officials and see what they think."

By four in the morning, Vinnie had copied all the video clips onto one VHS tape and gave it to Frank. Then Frank and Joe left the broadcast center. Joe was feeling good, the kind of good that settled in when he was just wrapping up a case.

"Hey, race you to the end of that path," Joe said to Frank, pointing ahead. "Then we can tell people we ran the 100-meter at the Olympics!"

"You're on," Frank said, taking off immediately.

Joe broke into a full-speed sprint and quickly passed his brother, charging ahead for all it was worth.

"Owwwwahhh!" Joe heard Frank cry out behind him. He turned around immediately.

"Frank!" Joe cried.

Frank was lying on the path near some bushes, doubled over in pain. Joe ran back to his brother and knelt in the grass beside him.

"Big mistake," a voice behind Joe said.

Joe whirled around just in time to see a tall, darkly clothed figure jump out of the shrubbery. The guy was about six-feet-two, with a muscular build. His face was covered with a black woolen ski mask.

"What's with the ski mask?" Joe said, starting to stand up. "It's a little early for the Winter Olympics."

But before Joe could say anything else, someone grabbed him from behind. It was an ambush! Two guys, not just one!

The one behind Joe was strong enough to twist Joe's right arm behind him and hold it there. "Don't move," he snarled. "Or I'll break you in pieces."

14 Moment of Truth

The grip on Joe's arm tightened, making pain shoot up into his shoulder. It was all the convincing Joe needed to keep still. In front of him, Frank rolled on the ground, still holding his stomach. With Frank down, the other guy stepped closer to Joe.

"It's time for you kids to learn a lesson," the guy in front of Joe said. "And I'm going to teach it to you."

Just then, Frank called out, "Hey, Joe, take a look behind you! On the other hand, why bother? The guy in front of you looks just the same."

"Shut up," ordered the guy standing behind Joe.

"No, really," Frank said, stumbling to his feet.

"These guys are dressed almost exactly alike. Hey, you don't think they're *twins*, do you?"

Joe felt a punch to his kidneys from the back. "Yeeow!" he cried. His legs wobbled. At the same time Joe felt his arm being twisted harder.

"Are you going to shut up or do you want to see me hit your brother again?" the voice behind Joe shouted.

Frank held up his hands, palms forward, to call a truce. "I guess you guys aren't in the mood for jokes."

Joe looked at the guy in front of him carefully, sizing him up. Frank was right. The guy was about Cory Conner's height. And he had Cory's taste in clothes, too. His designer jeans were perfectly pressed, and he was wearing expensive track shoes.

"What are we going to do with these punks who don't know how to stay out of other people's business?" the assailant said.

"Let's douse them in gasoline and throw them into the Olympic flame," the one behind Joe said.

"Hey, over there! Don't move!" a woman's voice called from across the grass. "This is security. You folks are trespassing on Olympic property. Hold it right there." The voice was getting louder with each word. Joe let out a sigh of relief.

As soon as the masked guys heard the guard coming, Joe's arm was released and they both ran.

Joe sagged. His back hurt and his arm was practically numb from lack of circulation.

"Are you okay?" Frank asked, rushing over to his brother.

The security officer came up with her flashlight in one hand and her billy club in the other. "What was that all about?" she asked.

"Just a little squabble between brothers," Frank quipped. "Could we use your walkie-talkie, please? We've got to get in touch with Cathleen Barton, and fast!"

It took a little convincing and a good long stare at the Hardys' credentials before the guard snapped into action. Within a few minutes, though, Frank and Joe were standing in Cathleen Barton's office again.

She looked at the videotape and listened to Frank explain his conclusions. "It's pretty sketchy evidence," Barton said finally. "But I happen to think you may be right. So I'll go out on the limb with you guys and let you present this to the Olympic Committee yourselves. I'll warn you, though," she added, "I'm going to call the Conners, too, and have them come as well. They deserve the right to defend themselves."

"No problem," Frank said. "All we need is a good night's sleep and we'll be ready."

"Okay," Cathleen said. "I want you back here at nine A.M."

As the Hardys walked back to their hotel, Joe

asked Frank, "Are you worried? Our evidence is pretty circumstantial."

"Worried doesn't begin to describe it," Frank replied. "If we're wrong, we could be in deep trouble."

"Let's just hope we're not," Joe said.

"Or that one of the twins confesses," Frank added.

The next morning Joe and Frank stepped out of the elevator into the third-floor reception area of the Olympic headquarters. Three tense security guards were standing there like a human wall, blocking the way.

"They're okay," Cathleen Barton called out. "Let them come in."

In addition to the regular security force, there were five men in suits, standing along the walls in the hall. They didn't need ID badges for Joe to know they were FBI, right down to their shiny shoes.

Agent McCracken was there, talking to Cathleen.

"Frank and Joe Hardy," he said, motioning for them to come over. They shook hands with the veteran FBI man again. He gave them a tight smile.

"Frank, the International Olympic Committee is waiting in that room." Barton pointed behind her. "Are you ready?" Frank nodded.

"Okay," McCracken said. "You boys go on in before the Conners arrive."

Frank took a deep breath and entered the long, wood-paneled office. Joe followed. Fifteen serious-faced men and women were seated around one side of a large oval wooden table. McCracken and Cathleen Barton sat down among them. The FBI agents took standing positions along the walls. Everyone was silent.

Cathleen Barton caught Frank's eye and nodded to the two chairs on the opposite side of the table. The chairs were placed beside a rolling cart with a VCR and a twenty-five-inch monitor for the Hardys to use.

Joe and Frank sat down and waited for Adam and Cory Conner to come in and take the remaining seats.

Finally the twins walked in. They looked identical, even down to the confident and slightly arrogant expressions on their faces—but they weren't dressed alike. Cory was wearing his TV network blue blazer, but Adam wore his United States Olympic uniform.

"Nice touch," Joe whispered to Frank. "I'm surprised he didn't wear his gold medal."

Cathleen and McCracken exchanged silent glances. She stood up at the head of the table. "Good morning. Before we start, it's important for everyone to understand that this is an investigative meeting—not a trial," she said. "I'd like to introduce Mr. Antonio Morreale, president of the International Olympic Committee."

A thin man, about fifty and wearing a stylish loose-fitting suit, stood up. Before he spoke, Morreale quickly smoothed a pencil-thin mustache under his nose. "Thank you all for coming. This is a very serious business," he said in a thick Italian accent. "We must hear all possible solutions to find out the truth. Please begin."

"Well, this is the short version," Frank said, standing up and moving toward the VCR controls. "We believe that Adam and Cory Conner are responsible for the notes threatening the Olympic Committee and marathon runners. However, the runners, and all of the athletes, were never in real danger because the notes were only part of a plot to cover up the fact that Cory substituted for Adam in two decathlon events."

Frank played the tape of Cory and Adam, explaining what each segment showed. He pointed out the events in which Adam appeared to start on his left foot instead of his right. Then he pointed out news segments in which Cory held the microphone in his right hand. Joe didn't watch the monitor, but kept his eyes trained on the twins, hoping to see them show their guilt. But the only thing he saw on their faces were looks of innocence. What about Morreale's face? Was he buying it? Who could tell?

Once Frank had played the entire tape, he

stopped the machine and said, "The only logical explanation for all this is that Cory and Adam traded places during the high-jump and the pole-vault events and then switched again. If you have any questions I'll try to answer them."

Frank sat down to dead silence. Cathleen looked at McCracken, who said nothing. She turned to Adam and Cory. "The committee will now hear your comments," she said.

"Our comments?" Cory fired back with a laugh. "I can't believe that you could possibly accuse us of doing something like this. Especially on the word of two kids."

"Their credentials in investigation are as strong as yours in athletics," Cathleen said. "So just stick to the evidence."

"What evidence—?" Adam began.

"It's insulting," Cory said, cutting his brother off. "Why did I hold the microphone in my right hand? You try holding a hand mike in the same hand for an hour. Your arm begins to cramp and your hand starts to shake, and that doesn't look too good on camera."

Cory rolled his eyes, as if he thought all the accusations were totally silly. And Joe and Frank could see that his performance was scoring points with the judges.

"Here's another great clue. He said that I was acting different or nervous during one report," Cory said. "Is that so strange? My brother was setting an Olympic record at the time. I *was* nervous—for him. I wanted to stop announcing and just shout, 'Go, Adam, go!' along with everyone else in the stadium.''

Joe couldn't take it anymore. "What about dumping chlorine in the Olympic pool?" he asked. "A witness spotted someone on the scene with a bathing suit like yours, Cory."

"You've got to be kidding," Adam said, speaking up. "Is my brother guilty just because of his bathing suit? No one said they specifically saw either of us at the pool. And as for my starting an event on one foot instead of the other, I'm a little weird because my style isn't consistent. But my coach will vouch for that."

This wasn't going right, Joe thought. The committee didn't believe Frank's evidence. The twins weren't about to confess. McCracken wasn't even listening anymore. He was writing something down in a small notebook he took from his jacket pocket.

"I'll tell you what hurts the most," Cory suddenly said. His voice was unsteady, as though he were about to break into tears. "I'd give anything to compete in the Olympics. It was my dream since I was a little kid, but I can't—not with this knee. All I can do is cheer for my brother to win. So if you think I'd do anything to distract people from watching him, you're nuts. I want everyone in the stadium to watch him and be

135

proud of him, proud of what he's doing for America."

Adam reached over and touched his brother's arm. "Thanks, Cory," he said.

There was another silence, and then the Olympic officials turned to each other and spoke quietly.

"Beautiful speech," Frank mumbled to Joe. "I just might cry."

Finally Mr. Morreale stood up again. "The committee believes," he said, "the evidence is circumstantial, coincidental, and entirely insufficient. We wish to extend our sincerest apologies to you, Adam and Cory, for this very embarrassing incident."

Joe knew if he looked over at Cathleen, she would be glaring at him. He did and she was.

"Don't you see the differences?" Frank said, pleading with them. He started the videotape again to show the officials one more time, but Cory cut him off.

"We've heard enough," Cory said. Both Conner brothers stood up and faced the Hardys. "I don't know what your problem is," Cory said, pointing a finger at Joe, "but if a word of any of this gets out to the public, we're suing you for everything. Right down to your shoelaces."

"Thanks," Joe said. "I don't know what I'd do without my shoelaces."

Cory and Adam stepped around the Hardys and were about to leave the room. Suddenly Frank stopped the tape recorder and jumped up to block their way.

"Wait just a second," he said. "I know you guys are guilty. And I can prove it!"

15 Video Proof

Frank stood his ground. He held up his hand, fingers spread. "I just need five more minutes," he said, moving his eyes to each of the Olympic officials in the room. Frank stared the hardest at Agent McCracken of the FBI and Mr. Morreale of the IOC. When his eyes met Cathleen Barton's he could read the question in her mind. "Can you really nail them?" Frank could hardly conceal his smile as he nodded to her.

Mr. Morreale rose and spoke again in his halting English. "Please, everyone, sit down for just five more minutes," he said.

"Thank you," Frank said, winking at Joe before addressing the group again. "Adam and Cory Conner are a special kind of identical twins called mirror-image twins," he said. He walked slowly, stopping to stand behind the brothers, who were sitting in two leather chairs. "They look alike, but Adam is right-handed while Cory is left-handed." Frank leaned in around the tall back of Cory's chair. "That's right, isn't it, Cory?"

Cory laughed. "Is this an investigation or a quiz?" he said.

"No, it's your funeral," Joe muttered under his breath.

Frank gave his brother a "keep-cool" glance. "I want to show part of the tape again, Joe," he said. "Play it with no sound till I tell you to stop it."

Joe hit "play" on the VCR. Everyone in the room watched Cory on the monitor one more time.

"Cory, you said that you didn't change your clothes during the second afternoon of the decathlon," Frank said.

"Yeah," Cory said, watching himself moving in fast motion on the screen.

"Before the hurdles you didn't change your shirt or tie or anything like that," Frank said.

Cory looked nervous but he answered with a strong no.

Frank stood behind Cory's chair. "You're absolutely positive?"

Cory turned around and stood up so that his face was only a few inches from Frank's. "How many times do I have to tell you? I didn't change anything! Adam and I didn't switch, okay?"

"Two minutes are up," said Agent McCracken.

"Stop the tape, Joe," Frank said calmly, turning away from Cory's face. He walked over and pointed to the screen as he spoke. "This is Cory during the second afternoon of the decathlon. Microphone in his left hand, hair neatly combed. Now, as we all know, left-handed people do things differently. They do everything left-handed—or backward, from a right-handed person's point of view."

"We've been through this," McCracken said sharply.

Frank quickly turned back to the screen. "If you look carefully at Cory's necktie in this shot, you'll see the slant at the top of the knot goes down from his left to his right, the way any left-handed person would tie a tie. Now run the tape up, Joe, to Cory's interview later that day."

There was a murmur through the audience in the spacious office while Joe ran through the tape. They were expecting something big, and Frank knew he wouldn't disappoint them.

"Stop," Frank told Joe. "Here's Cory on camera forty minutes later—at the exact moment the pole-vaulting competition is taking place. He's holding the microphone in his right hand now and his hair is a little messy. We already knew that. What I didn't notice until a few minutes ago was the knot in his tie."

Joe put his face close to the screen. "The slant is going down from right to left," he said in amazement.

"The way a right-handed person would tie a tie," Frank said. "Cory, you told us just now that you didn't change your clothes. So the only logical explanation for why your tie is different here is because this isn't you. It's Adam."

Cory sagged in his chair. Adam slumped forward. Here and there in the room there were small gasps and soft murmurs. Frank saw that McCracken's face had cracked a small smile. Cathleen Barton was beaming.

"I don't believe it," Cory said, shaking his head. "We've worked this out for three years. How could we have overlooked that?"

"Don't admit anything," Adam said, shooting his brother a glare.

"Why not?" Cory said. "They've got us."

"The less they know, the better it'll be for us," Adam said.

"Don't count on that," said Agent McCracken, getting out of his seat. He pulled out a small cassette recorder and pushed the record button. "Talk. Cooperation scores points with us."

Adam sat back heavily in his chair.

"Look, it was my idea," Cory said. "I thought of it three years ago, when I hurt my knee. I recovered completely, but I kept it quiet because I thought, well, Adam never was a good jumper. We've traded places all our lives. It's something twins do. I thought, hey, decathlon time! If I trained for Adam's two weak events, the high jump and the pole vault, we couldn't lose! I talked Adam into this scheme, and I've been training secretly for three years."

A smile started to come across Cory's face, but he stifled it fast. "We even switched in competitions just to see if we could get away with it. We had even the coaches fooled. They thought Adam was ambidextrous."

Cathleen Barton rose to her feet, eager to get all the facts. "But why did you want to sabotage the Olympics?"

The Conners looked at each other, and then Adam cleared his throat. His face was tight. "That was my idea," he said. "I was nervous about going through with this, even though we've been switching places in competitions. This was the Olympics! The whole world was watching. I thought we had to do something to focus media attention away from us. Otherwise, the decathlon was going to get too much coverage, and I figured we'd get caught."

"Go on," said Agent McCracken.

Adam looked at Cory and went on. "I got the idea when the IOC mailed the room-assignment sheets to all the athletes. If we made a threat against some other competition, maybe that would take the focus off us. We picked the marathon, since that event was taking place at the same time Cory was doing the pole vault. We also

142

mailed the first threat to the committee and followed it with notes to the marathoners. Cory just slipped the notes under their doors late one night."

"But why pour oil in the Olympic flame, put chlorine in the pool, and oil the high bar?" Cathleen said. "Didn't you care what happened to your fellow athletes?"

Cory shifted uncomfortably on his chair. "Sure, but we had to make people believe in the threat, see?"

"Just tell us how you did it," said Agent McCracken. "The Olympic flame."

"That was me," Adam admitted. "I was running the stadium stairs for exercise with a lot of athletes. I put oil in my water bottle, and poured that in, then added some explosives. It took several trips to do the job.

"The swimming pool?" McCracken asked flatly.

"That was me using Adam's ID," Cory said. He tapped his thumbs nervously on the table in front of him. "I just dropped a plastic bucket of highly concentrated chlorine in the pool."

"We knew no one would get hurt with these stunts," Adam added.

"I'm sure that was the last thing Kyung Chin was expecting," Frank said, not trying to hide the edge in his voice.

"Yeah, I oiled the bar early one morning, after the crew had set up the gymnastic equipment,"

Cory said. "It was easy to get in there with my press credentials, and no one was around. I'm real sorry about Kyung. We're not killers, you know."

"No, you just like to deliver poison cakes and drain gas tanks so people get stuck on railroad tracks," Joe snapped.

"Let's stick to the facts, please," said Agent McCracken. "What about this poison cake?"

Cory squirmed in his seat. "We have a cousin who lives here," Adam said. "He's a vet. He gave us something he uses to knock out animals."

McCracken shook his head and wrote something more down in his notebook.

"And as for draining your gas tank," Adam went on, turning to Joe. "We were just trying to keep you guys away from Sports City. We followed you from the river to that restaurant. I guess we didn't drain all your gas, even though we planned to."

"I have another question," Frank said. "How did you know where to find us last night?"

"The receptionist at the broadcast center is a friend of mine," Cory said. "I told her to call me if you guys started nosing around again."

Frank paced the room silently. The Olympic officials looked shocked, confused, and angry. President Morreale shook his head sadly. McCracken was impatient to haul the Conners away, and Cathleen Barton's face looked relieved to have this one wrapped up.

But it was the look on the Conners' faces that

144

surprised him the most. Cory and Adam seemed to realize for the first time what they had done. The truth was melting them from the inside out.

Agent McCracken made a quick hand motion, and three agents quickly handcuffed Adam and Cory and took them from the room. No one said a word until they were gone. Then Agent McCracken shook hands with Cathleen Barton and headed for the door.

"Pretty slick work," he said. He walked past Frank and Joe without looking at them, closing the door behind him.

"Regulation FBI compliment," Joe muttered under his breath to Frank.

"Thank you indeed, Frank and Joe," said Mr. Morreale, coming over to shake hands. "This is a sad day for the Olympics. It would have been much sadder, however, not to have found out the truth." He turned to the committee members around the table. "Now, we must face the decision of how to tell the world what has happened."

Frank figured that was their cue to leave. He caught Joe's eye and motioned to the door. Cathleen Barton left, too, and they all stood in the hall outside the conference room.

"A couple of chips off the old block," she said. "Fenton Hardy would be proud. Everything tied up in your minds?"

"Sure," Joe said, looking over at Frank.

"We took some wrong turns," Frank said. "We suspected the wrong athletes for a while—Chili

Pepper Morgan, Sigrid Randers-Perhson, and Mad Dog."

Cathleen smiled.

"Yeah," Joe added, "we even thought maybe someone pushed us when we fell in the stadium stands. But I guess we were just pushed by the crowds."

"Speaking of crowds," Cathleen said, "I'll bet there's a gang of reporters outside the building—newspapers, TV, radio, everything you can imagine—waiting to get the whole story. They've been shadowing me since yesterday. I want you two right next to me. We're going to look like heroes, and you guys should get your share."

"I can live with that," Joe said, beaming.

"The truth is, I owe you guys," Cathleen said. "If there's something I can do for you, let me know."

"Well," Joe said, "as a matter of fact, we heard there's a private party for all the athletes after the closing ceremonies. It would be really cool if we could go."

"Consider yourselves invited," Cathleen said. "I'll have three passes delivered to your hotel this afternoon."

"How did you know we needed three?" Frank asked.

"I'm not head of security for nothing," she said. With a smile, she held her walkie-talkie to her mouth to answer a call.

Just then the elevator door opened, and Chet and Sean stepped out. As soon as they saw Frank and Joe they came rushing over. Chet had his camera in hand, clicking away.

"Well done, lads," Sean said, pushing his sunglasses up onto his forehead. "You should see the crowd that's building up downstairs. Everyone wants to hear your story."

"Did you see Cory and Adam down there?" Joe asked.

"Yeah," Chet said. "I got some great pictures of them getting into an FBI car."

"Chet," Frank said, "you're going to have a great photo album, but you must have spent a fortune on film this week."

"Not exactly," Chet said, stopping to think. "I only bought one roll."

"Only one roll?" Joe sputtered. "But you've taken hundreds of pictures! Didn't you change the film?"

Chet's face turned pale. "I was so busy," he said. "I knew I was forgetting to do something, but I couldn't remember what." He practically tore open the back of his camera to look inside.

Frank's eyes bulged with surprise. "There's no film in there at all?"

Then Chet sheepishly took a new, unopened roll of film out of his jeans pocket. "Load the camera—*that's* what I forgot!"

"Say, guys," Cathleen said, moving back toward them, "I couldn't help overhearing this little drama, and I think I can help. How about if I arrange a private photo session with your favorite athletes for you?"

"Wow! That would be super," Chet said. Then he put his arm around Sean's shoulder. "My favorite athlete is right here."

"Are you ready to meet the press, guys?" Cathleen asked. Frank and Joe nodded, and she hit the elevator call button.

"Say, Frank," Chet said, looking at his empty camera. "Does this mean that you're not going to call me a genius anymore?"

Frank thought for a minute. "Okay, Chet, we'll still call you a genius," he said, giving him a slap on the back. "But there's one thing we'll never call you."

"Thanks—uh, what's that?" Chet asked.

"A photographer!"

THE HARDY BOYS® SERIES   By Franklin W. Dixon

NANCY DREW® MYSTERY STORIES By Carolyn Keene